P9-DHG-437

SHADOW GRAVE

ALSO BY MARINA COHEN

The Inn Between
The Doll's Eye
A Box of Bones

SHADOW GRAVE

MARINA COHEN

Roaring Brook Press
New York

Published by Roaring Brook Press
Roaring Brook Press is a division of Holtzbrinck Publishing
Holdings Limited Partnership
120 Broadway, New York, NY 10271 • fiercereads.com

Our books may be purchased in bulk for promotional, educational,
or business use. Please contact your local bookseller or the Macmillan
Corporate and Premium Sales Department at (800) 221-7945 ext. 5442
or by email at MacmillanSpecialMarkets@macmillan.com.

Library of Congress Cataloging-in-Publication Data is available.

First edition, 2022

Book design by Trisha Previte.
Leaves and doll illustrations © by Hannah Peck.
Chapter header illustration by Trisha Previte.
Printed in the United States of America by LSC Communications,
Harrisonburg, Virginia

ISBN 978-1-250-78300-4

1 3 5 7 9 10 8 6 4 2

For Auntie Anna, in loving memory

PART ONE

THE ROAD TO LIVERMORE

Civilization dwindled.

First the towns—tiny clusters of homes, steeples, and storefronts. Then the farms, with sagging barns and gray silos reaching into a gunpowder sky. And finally the road, which disappeared as pavement crumbled to gravel that crunched beneath the tires of the old maroon Buick.

Arlo Davis cranked the passenger window. A chilly breeze wafted into the car. He filled his lungs with crisp fall air and peered out at the bleak countryside.

"I think we took a wrong turn."

The cornfields on either side lay fallow. Ribbons of fog snaked along the earth dotted with broken, bent stalks, shriveled brownish-gold leaves, and the skeletal remains of tractors, plows, and combines.

"Perfect setting for a zombie apocalypse!" announced Lola from the back seat.

Heather Flores frowned. "Have you been letting your sister watch that silly show when I'm at work?"

"*Zombie Army of Darkness* is not silly," said Lola. "It's only the most watched drama in basic cable history."

"She has a point," said Arlo.

His mother's gaze bobbled from the road to Arlo, then back to the road. "She's too young," she muttered. "It's too scary. She should be watching happy shows. Like *Rainbow Wonders* or *Unicorn Utopia*."

Lola leaned forward, her seat belt stretching to its limits. "I'm almost nine. I'm never scared. And I hate unicorns."

Arlo had to hand it to his little sister. He'd have been terrified of all those decrepit and decomposing bodies when he was her age. Truth be told, at twelve years old, he still was.

He preferred to watch the Nature Channel. He was more interested in biology and botany than brain eaters. But all his friends watched *Zombie Army of Darkness*, and he didn't want to be left out of the conversation, so he made sure to catch every episode.

He gave his mother an earnest look. "She *is* pretty tough. Like you."

His mother tapped her periwinkle fingernails on the steering wheel, sighed, and shook her head. Her long red curls swayed. Arlo made a sour face. He couldn't get used to that color. He liked her brown hair.

"You're tough, too," she said. "In a different way."

Arlo wished that were true. His mother was always trying to make light of things. Make him feel better about himself. Less anxious. More at ease.

The car radio was tuned to an increasingly static station that proudly proclaimed to play *all oldies, all the time*. A high-pitched voice screeched a solitary line over and over as if skipping on an old vinyl record.

"This thing isn't working." Arlo poked the portable GPS screen. "It's supposed to *provide driver alerts to increase awareness*. There've been tons of sharp turns, and it hasn't warned us. Not once." He jabbed harder, but the device remained steady and silent. "We should have used Waze."

"We don't have good reception here—the app would have cut out." She took her hand off the wheel and adjusted the rearview mirror.

"B-Both hands on the wheel!" Arlo sputtered. "Ten o'clock! Two o'clock!" He was years away from driving, but he had already studied the online driver's manual.

His mother tousled his curly black hair and returned

her hand to the wheel. "Relax, Arlo. Remember what Dr. Lewis said? Positive thoughts."

"Yeah," echoed Lola. "Positive thoughts." She punched his upper arm.

He turned and glared. Lola batted her eyelashes and then leaned back, placing her dirty soccer cleats on his headrest. She powered up her tablet and plugged in her earbuds.

It was their mother's idea to book an old Federal-style mansion bed-and-breakfast on the East Coast for Thanksgiving. They were going to *leave the world behind*. No TV. Take long walks, eat chowder, and get plenty of ocean air. It was a long drive for a few days. To make matters worse, she refused to take the interstate.

Arlo glanced at the sky. It was a brooding menace. "We're not going to make it before dark."

"Well, at least we'll be able to say we took *the road less traveled . . .*" She dropped her voice for dramatic effect. "*And that has made all the difference.*"

Arlo took his phone out of his pocket and began filming the landscape. Cornfields had given way to a struggling apple orchard. Remnants of rotting fruit lay strewn beneath bare and baleful branches. The air suddenly smacked of cider and hayrides.

"I don't think that's what he meant."

His mother fiddled with the radio, more static than song. She tried the tuner. All stations crackled in and out, so she switched it off altogether.

"Huh?"

"The poem you were quoting," said Arlo. "'The Road Not Taken'—it's by Robert Frost."

He zoomed in on a derelict greenhouse. Like a long-forgotten glass castle left to decay, its windows were shattered, its metal frame rusted and tilting. Monstrous vegetation grew rampant through the jagged openings. A huge maple burst through the roof.

"Since when are you a poetry expert?"

Arlo stopped filming. He tried to upload the footage to his social story, but the connection kept breaking. "Mr. Kim read it to us. Along with a bunch of others." He concealed all trace of enthusiasm, but truthfully, he had rather enjoyed the poetry unit.

"Mr. Kim." She smiled. "Can't believe that old guy hasn't retired. He must be a hundred."

"He says the poem is about two roads. And the narrator has to pick one."

"Hate to tell you this, Bud, but that's pretty obvious."

"Yes," said Arlo, "but most people think it's about choosing the better way. The right way. *The road less traveled*. Like, not following the crowd. Freethinking. All that stuff."

"Exactly. That's why I like it."

Arlo fidgeted with his phone. His carrier indicator kept flickering to No Service. He stole a backward glance. He could still see the brittle branches of the maple reaching toward the sky like a petrified giant surrendering to the clouds. He closed the window. The vent coughed stale air into his face.

"Mr. Kim says the poem isn't about decision at all. It's about indecision."

His mother cocked her head. "How does he figure?"

"He said it doesn't really matter which path you choose—so long as you choose. When Frost says it *made all the difference*, he was being ironic."

His mother pondered this for a moment. "You know, you're pretty smart for a sixth grader. Though . . ." She dragged the word a little too long for his liking. "You did say we took a wrong turn. If there is no right way, then there's no wrong way. Kind of ironic, dontcha think?"

Arlo narrowed his eyes. She had a point.

His mother was only thirty, but her face seemed older. Every year was etched into her features, weighed down by worry she tried hard to mask. She hadn't finished high school—had to quit to have him, get a job to support him—yet she was the smartest person he knew. She could calculate the most difficult math problem in her head, reassemble a broken toaster in a matter of minutes, and recite the entire national anthem backward.

She could have been anything. A nuclear physicist. A brain surgeon. Instead, she'd married his father, Milton Davis, had Lola, and now worked at a dusty desk in a crumbling building.

She was smarter than his father, the podiatrist, who Lola liked to call the *toenail trimmer*, the *corn chopper*, or the *bunion butcher*. He didn't appreciate her humor.

Arlo's father had a new wife, Renée, and new baby, Reginald. Arlo and Lola only got to see little Reggie on alternate weekends. Babies were a lot of work, so it made sense he had even less time for them these days.

They passed a sign with lettering that proudly announced WELCOME, NEW HAMPSHIRE. Arlo read the slogan at the bottom out loud. "Live free or die."

"The phrase is attributed to John Stark—a New Hampshire general," said his mother. "But it was actually adapted from the French Revolution—*Vivre libre ou mourir!*"

Arlo frowned. There was something about the sentiment he didn't quite understand. It seemed somehow extreme.

Arlo stuffed his phone into his pocket, leaned back in the seat, and closed his eyes. When he opened them again, the sky had grown darker and a mist had blown in, washing the world of color. The peaks of the mountains vanished behind a hazy curtain of twilight.

Arlo's mother reached a hand behind the passenger seat and held it out. Lola fished a bag of Larry's Licorice Laces—Spearmint Green—from a plastic grocery bag filled with chips, chocolate, and Little Debbie Happy Camper Cakes.

"Robert Frost lived around here," his mother said, taking the bag and flipping it into Arlo's lap. "For a while."

They made a sharp turn, zipped past a water park— SPLISH! SPLASH!—its slides abandoned for the season, and then a campground devoid of tents and RVs. They were in *the North Country* now.

Pine, oak, beech, ash, and hemlock crowded either side of the road. The trunks grew thicker and taller. Above, the strip of sky diminished little by little until it disappeared altogether.

Arlo had watched an episode of *Tree Planet* that featured old-growth forests. Though he hadn't thought trees this enormous existed anymore, especially at this altitude.

How old were they? One hundred? One thousand?

There was a photo in his textbook of a tree somewhere in California that was five thousand years old. What would it be like to live five thousand years? Would you get bored?

"I'm sure we're going the wrong way." Arlo yanked open the plastic and held it toward his mother.

She withdrew two rubbery strands of green licorice—*Four Feet of Fun!*—and stuffed one into her mouth.

"Did you know New Hampshire is home to ten National Register of Champion Trees—the largest of their species nationwide?" he said, but neither his mother nor Lola were listening.

He had no idea why they were even taking the trip. It came out of nowhere. They always spent Thanksgiving with Grandma Pearl, but his mother had insisted. She said they needed some *time away together*. They were together all the time.

Lola rummaged through the cooler, found a red apple, and offered it to Arlo. He waved it away. He could hear her take a large bite of the crisp fruit while his mother chewed the spearmint laces.

"How can you eat that stuff? It tastes like toothpaste."

The car trundled over an old set of railroad tracks. Ahead, Arlo noticed a fork in the road. An old splintered sign pointed to the right. The script was missing. In the dim light, all he could make out was the letter *L* and the number *8*.

Keep left, announced the cheerful electronic voice of the GPS. His mother veered left.

"It's not natural. It's practically neon. You know Japan and Germany ban those food colors?"

She stuffed the second piece into her mouth. "I like it."

"It can't be healthy. It could make you—"

He caught himself just in time. His eyes darted toward his mother. She didn't flinch, but she paused a moment and then chewed a lot slower.

It's going to be okay.

His mother's words, spoken so long ago, were like earworms burrowing deep into his brain, going round and round.

He wanted to say he was sorry, that he didn't mean to say anything upsetting, but he wouldn't have the chance.

Everything happened at once, though the events seemed to unfold in slow-motion play. Time and space stretched long and thin like an elastic band, and Arlo had the strange sensation he was watching it on a movie screen.

Something leaped out of the woods and landed smack-dab in the middle of the road. It was a massive blur of horns and fur and limbs. Before Arlo's brain could catch up to his eyes, he heard a sickening thud. A shatter of glass, and a million shards flew at him like a swarm of angry bees.

His hands flew to his face instinctively, and he shut his eyes. The car lurched, tearing up dirt and gravel on the side of the road as it slid. They spun forever, lost somewhere in the space-time continuum.

Then the elastic band reached its limits and snapped back.

The car hammered into something solid with the force of an atomic bomb. There was a concert of crunching metal. A chorus of clangs. A symphony of screeches. Arlo's mind exploded with color and pain and noise and then . . .

Someone hit the Mute button, and the world around him spiraled into darkness.

A pebble of awareness fell into the deep, dark pool inside Arlo's mind. It formed a ripple. Then, gradually, one by one, more ripples spread lazily outward, nudging him, prodding him, until at last, he emerged from the murky depths into a dim consciousness.

He tried several times to open his eyes but failed, so he remained still for some time, drifting in and out of nothingness, his senses struggling to form a solid thought.

Am I dead? he wondered.

It was a definite possibility. Then his fingertips began to prickle, his head to throb. Around him, he became aware of sounds and smells. The *scritch, scratch* of claws scuttling up coarse bark. The hoot of an owl. The musky scent of decomposing vegetation, mingling with the pungent odor of battery fluid and gasoline.

His eyelids flickered open, and for a moment, he didn't know where he was. He scoured his memory. He had been in the car. He and his mother had been talking. Lola had taken a bite of an apple, and then . . .

The memory came back to him like a knife to the chest. Panic filled his lungs. He coughed and gasped for air, but there wasn't enough oxygen in the whole world to fill even half his lungs.

Arlo had no idea how long he'd been unconscious, but something had changed. Dusk had given way to a thick, downy darkness. Only a drizzle of moonlight penetrated the dense forest, creating lacy patterns where it pooled on the ground. He swallowed his sobs, gathered his wits, and did his best to quiet his fear.

He was not dead. But what about the others?

"Mom?" he said in a hoarse whisper. "Lo?"

The words sent puffs of vapor into the night air. It was cold. The temperature had dropped. Mist on the car had frozen to a thin layer of crystals. They formed delicate designs that glistened like a thousand gemstones where they caught the moonlight.

His body was stiff and sore, but he managed to turn his head and discovered the shape of his mother slumped over the steering wheel. He lifted an arm and winced. He touched her back and jiggled.

"Mom? Are you okay?"

At first, there was no response, and a second wave of panic coursed through his veins. He shook her again, this time more fervently. At last, she stirred and groaned, and he breathed a sigh.

Turning his head as far as he could manage, he couldn't locate his sister. "Lola? Lo?" he called. "Lo? Where are you?"

There was a pause that lasted an eternity. Then he heard her.

"Over . . . here," she said between ragged breaths, her voice coming from somewhere outside the car.

Arlo lowered his head and closed his eyes. He said a silent prayer. His mother was alive. Lola was alive. They were all alive. And for that brief moment, it was all that mattered.

When he opened his eyes again, he began to assess the damage. The front of the car was a total wreck. They had hit a massive tree—the biggest he'd ever seen—head-on.

The windshield had been shattered, the hood of the car crumpled like an old paper bag, and the engine mangled. Luckily, he had not been impaled by an enormous low-hanging branch that pointed toward him like an accusing finger.

Arlo fumbled for his seat belt and undid it. It was a

good thing he had been wearing one, or he'd have been tossed through the windshield like an old rag doll.

He opened the door and tumbled out onto the cold, hard ground. Every inch of him ached, but at least he could move. His muscles felt like they were on fire.

Grunting with the effort, he slowly raised himself to a standing position, dusted off his knees, and then rubbed his neck. Other than a tear in his sweatshirt near the waist and a few cuts to his hands and face, he appeared intact. He was bruised more than broken.

The passenger door was ajar. He found Lola sitting on the ground on the side of the road, her back against a tree, hugging her knees to her chest, her head bent, her hair raining down onto her denim overalls in a cascade of curls.

He hobbled toward her. "Hey, Lo? You okay?"

She lifted her head slowly. Her eyes met his. They were large and doe-like. She nodded. "I think so. How's Mom?"

"She seems all right." He limped around the back of the car toward the driver's side. Liquid was dripping beneath the carriage. Gas and antifreeze glistened blue in the moonlight.

His mother leaned back in her seat. Her red wig had come off, revealing patchy brown hair. Her face was waxy and pale. There was a large goose egg on her forehead, and her nose and lip were crusted with drops of dried blood. He opened her door and tugged at her until she became more alert.

"What happened?" she said groggily.

"We had an accident. Are you okay?"

She groaned and lifted her left leg out of the wreckage. It was only when she brought her right foot into view and choked back a yelp that Arlo noticed the ankle was slightly askew.

At first, he thought it odd she was wearing one black shoe and one red. Then his body tensed. It wasn't a red shoe at all. She sunk back down into the driver's seat. "I'm fine. Where's Lo?"

"Over here," said his sister. She hadn't moved from her spot.

"She's shaken, but okay," he said encouragingly. He grappled inside his pocket for his phone. The screen was cracked, but it turned on. Blue light blasted his face.

It was after 3 A.M. He'd been passed out for hours. He tried to call 911 but couldn't get a signal. He attempted several times, shifting about to try and get reception, then finally gave up and stuffed the phone back into his pocket.

"You're bleeding," he said. "You need help." Even as he spoke the words, he knew there was none to be had.

She looked down at her foot almost absentmindedly. "It's not so bad." Her voice was soft and unalarmed, as though she hadn't yet fully grasped their predicament. She held up her phone. It was shattered.

"Oh, darn," she said, seeing her hand. "Broke a nail." She tossed her phone aside, shifted her foot, and Arlo saw the skin was peeled back, the white of bone peeking through knots of gristle and sinew.

His stomach gave a violent jump. He backed away and was sick in the ferns on the side of the road. There was a sharp noise echoing around him. Someone was screaming. Dragging a sleeve across his mouth, he realized the screams had been coming from him. He clamped his jaw, inhaling deeply through his nostrils.

"What's wrong?" said Lola, racing up from behind. "Why are you screaming?"

With his external voice muzzled, his inner voice took control. His mother was injured. She needed his help. After everything they'd been through the past year, he wasn't about to let her down now.

"Mom's injured," he said. "We have to help her."

Lola took a deep breath and nodded.

Luckily, in the fourth grade, Arlo's teacher, Ms. MacLean, had taken the class on a wilderness outing. Prior to going, his father had insisted he take a first aid course. Arlo had learned how to do the Heimlich maneuver—abdominal thrusts—how to perform CPR, how to deal with minor burns and cuts, and how to control bleeding. His memory was fuzzy as he struggled to recall the training.

Step one: Stop the bleeding with a bandage, sterile cloth, or piece of clothing.

Arlo made a beeline for the car. Lola followed.

"It's all right," his mother kept murmuring. "Don't worry . . ."

He managed to open the trunk and got out his suitcase. In it he found a white T-shirt and began tearing it apart at the seams. Together, he and Lola ripped it into strips.

Once they had enough, they raced back to their mother. She cried out only once while Arlo wrapped the break tightly.

Step two: Immobilize the injured area.

Arlo turned to Lola. "Stay with her." He returned to his suitcase and got out his extra pair of sneakers. Quick as lightning, he removed the laces and then began searching the side of the road for fallen branches straight enough to create a splint.

The darkness made the task all the more difficult, but

he managed to find two such sticks. He was about to head back to the car when something caught his eye.

It lay in the ditch a few feet away, glistening in a patch of moonlight. At first, it looked like an oddly shaped branch. He took a step toward it. Like the up-reaching palm of a mythical beast lay the single antler of a massive animal.

A deer, Arlo thought at first, but it was enormous, and with its butterfly-wing shape, it most likely belonged to an elk or a moose. He knew moose shed their paddles in winter. Arlo tried to lift it, but the paddle must have weighed twenty pounds or more.

He heard the soft snap of a twig and dropped the antler. There was a stain in the shadows. He thought he glimpsed something enormous and misshapen hidden in folds of misty gloom. He half expected a one-paddled moose to burst from the darkness. He blinked, and the shadow was gone.

Arlo rushed back to his mother, carrying the sturdy sticks. A dark spot was visible through the T-shirt on her ankle, but it was not getting too large too quickly. The bleeding was slowing, he thought. That was good.

"I'm going to make a splint," he said to Lola, "but I need your help. Hold these in place." She nodded and then he placed the branches on either side of his mother's ankle. While Lola held them firmly, Arlo spiraled the shoelaces one at a time around the area, tying each off in a tight knot.

"Wow," said their mother. "I'm impressed."

Step three: *Apply ice.*

He opened the other passenger door. The cooler had flipped onto its side, but the lid was still secure. The ice had not fully melted.

"Grab another T-shirt," he instructed Lola. She raced to the back of the car and returned in a flash with one from his already open suitcase. He filled the cloth with ice and then tied it off.

"Elevate the injury above the heart," he said as if reciting from an instruction manual.

Both he and Lola supported their mother's weight as they moved her from the front seat to the back. They helped her maneuver herself so that her leg was up on the driver's seat they'd tilted forward. Arlo placed the makeshift ice bag over her ankle.

Step four: *Treat for shock.*

Arlo found a wooly sweater in her suitcase and placed it around his mother's shoulders. Then he located her jacket and draped that over her as well. "Keep the victim warm."

The word *warm* triggered something inside Arlo. He realized for the first time he was shivering. He couldn't tell if it was the cold or his nerves. He found both his and Lola's jackets in the back seat. He pulled his on and zipped it up. Clinging to what heat his body could muster, he handed Lola her jacket.

He stood back and for a moment allowed a small bit of pride to swell in his heart. He had done this. All by himself. His father would be so proud of him. Then he remembered there was one final directive:

Seek help.

Arlo tried his phone again. He managed to get a single bar and got excited for a moment, but before he could even open his phone app, it flashed back to no signal.

Perhaps another car might come along. He stood in the center of the road. It stretched away from him, disappearing into darkness in either direction. There was no glimmer of approaching headlights, no distant rumble of an engine. He recalled how they had driven several miles on that road prior to the accident without encountering so much as a single vehicle. What were the chances one would come along at this late hour?

He kicked at the gravel so hard he nearly injured his own foot. "*Darn road less traveled.*"

He booted the ground a few more times and then,

taking a few deep breaths, he headed back to the car, plunked himself down on the cooler, and sat worrying. With the rush of adrenaline gone, the aches and pains returned, and a dizziness overcame him. He leaned over and cradled his head in his hands.

"Are you sure you're all right?" asked his mother, reaching out to comfort him. "You don't look well."

"I'm fine," he lied, running a hand through his hair.

She didn't seem convinced. "What did we hit?" she asked, as if the thought had struck her quite suddenly.

"A tree," said Lola.

Their mother shook her head. "Before that."

Arlo thought for a moment. There *had* been something else. Something large and furry. He remembered the paddle he'd seen in the ditch, perhaps shed, perhaps torn, once maybe velvety soft, now like a piece of brown bone.

"Moose, I think. Pretty big one."

"Moose? Poor thing," she sighed. "Hope we didn't hurt it."

"I hope not," he said.

Arlo knew moose were massive creatures. They had a powerful kick that could destroy most predators. Yet they could be done in by a single bite, or gash, if it got infected. If they'd hit a moose, they'd certainly injured it. Perhaps even lethally.

He looked at his mother's ankle. If it got infected, she'd go the same way as the moose. They couldn't just sit there waiting for help that might never arrive.

Arlo stood. He headed back into the forest of tall trees, their trunks covered in fungi and lichen, their roots woven together like bird nests. He'd been in many forests, but none like this. None so deep and dark and old.

He didn't search long before he found what he needed. He returned to the car carrying a large branch with a V at one end. It would make a decent enough crutch. He carefully stripped it clean.

"We need to go," he said to his mother gently. "Do you think you can walk?"

"Like a champ," she said, forcing a smile that quickly turned into a wince.

He reached under her arm and helped her stand. "I saw a sign not far back. There could be a town that way. It's our best bet."

"Hang on," she said, and found the plastic bag of treats. "For the road." She smiled.

Arlo tried to smile back, but he couldn't make his mouth form the proper shape.

Using the crutch to support her weight, they began to pick a careful path back the way they came. With each step, Arlo's uneasiness grew.

He scanned the forest, and though it was dark, all his senses conspired, and it seemed to him there was something in the shadows, just beyond the tendrilled-reach of moonlight. He looked away, but it was there, fluttering at the edges of his peripheral vision—threatening to dissolve if he were to look at it head-on.

The forest felt strange. The tree limbs were thick and twisted and pointed at odd angles. Gnarled roots, like black veins, coiled out of the crumbling earth. It had a hostile, almost otherworldly quality, and Arlo felt like he had to speak louder and more frequently to break its spell.

"Do you need to rest? I can try and find a better crutch. Here—lean on me."

"I'm fine," said his mother. It was the same thing she'd said after each of the treatments.

He'd been so relieved when at last she was given a clean bill of health. So grateful it was all behind them. Compared to what she had gone through the previous year, a broken bone was nothing. If she could just get proper care, a broken bone would heal in no time.

His mother hobbled forward gingerly. Arlo did his best to slow himself to keep to her pace while Lola took the lead. The stiffness in Arlo's limbs had diminished, but he was still riddled with dull aches. It was slow going, but finally they made it to the fork in the road.

Arlo held up his phone and shone the flashlight function on the wooden sign. Up close, he could make out the shadow of lettering that had been stripped by time.

Town of Livermore

Est. 1876

He checked for a phone signal—still no service—and then switched off the device. He didn't want to drain the already low battery. Darkness gobbled up the surroundings and swallowed the sign.

"Maybe this isn't such a good idea," he said. "Maybe we should keep going along the road and try and find a farmhouse."

"There's nothing but an empty campground and closed water park that way," said Lola.

"She's right," said his mother. "At least this is a town. There will be phone service. And help."

Arlo gazed one way down the dark road, then looked

back the way they had come. Disquiet bloomed in his chest. He sighed and dispelled it. "Okay. Livermore it is."

His mother took a few steps, and then paused. "I just hope they're not famous for their chopped liver."

"I dunno," said Arlo. "I kind of like chopped liver."

Lola narrowed her eyes skeptically. "Since when?"

"Since Ethan made me try it. It's really good."

"And you think Larry's Licorice Laces taste awful . . ." His mother chuckled.

As she walked, her stick scraped along the gravel carpeted in deadfall. The grocery bag swished side to side.

To call it a road was overly optimistic. The way to Livermore began wide enough, but with each passing step, it narrowed until, a mile or so along, it had diminished to little more than an overgrown footpath—a rabbit trail through a forest so overgrown it was more like a tunnel than a path. Had it not been for the sign, Arlo would have sworn it was leading them nowhere. Had they not traveled this far, he'd have certainly turned back.

Arlo hadn't always been this anxious. His mother's illness had taken its toll on him as well. It had changed him as much as it had changed her. He wasn't an altogether different person, just a muted, more tentative version of his former self.

Dr. Lewis had diagnosed him with anxiety, and his

treatment included replacing negative thoughts with positive ones. Arlo gazed at the surrounding woods, a thousand shades of black. It was cold, and getting colder. The car was a wreck. His mother was badly injured. And there might or might not be a town up ahead. Arlo tried his best, but he could find nothing positive about their situation.

"Little Debbie?" asked his mother, pausing to fish a treat from her grocery bag. Propping herself on the crutch, she unwrapped a tree-shaped cake smothered in green frosting and handed it to Lola. She unwrapped a second and offered it to Arlo.

"What's with you and green food color?" he said.

"Makes me feel closer to nature."

Arlo's gaze swept the curtain of trunks and low-hanging branches. For a second, he imagined something flitted from shadow to shadow. Then all was still.

"I feel a little too close to nature as is," he mumbled, ripping off a hunk of the chocolate cake and popping it in his mouth. He let his mother have the rest.

Vaporous puffs burst from Arlo's mouth and nostrils as they began trekking again along the narrow path. There was no snow—not yet—but the earth had grown hard. Bare trees were rimed with frost, moisture crystallized on dead leaves, and puddles were turning to black ice. If it did snow, he thought with a sudden panic, a whole lot, it might cover the car and there would be no evidence of the accident. No proof they were here.

It's going to be okay.

He zipped up his jacket as far as it would go and hugged his chest, wishing he'd brought the wool cap and gloves he'd packed. His teeth began to chatter.

"Take my jacket," offered his mother. "Throw it over yours. I've got the wool sweater."

"You can have mine," said Lola. "I'm not cold. I've got iguana blood."

"Iguanas don't like the cold," said Arlo. "They're cold-blooded, but they become immobile when the temperature falls below a certain level. At fifty degrees, they're sluggish. Under forty, their blood stops moving altogether."

"Oh yeah," said Lola. "I remember the year it got so cold in Florida the TV reporter said it was raining iguanas. They were literally dropping out of trees."

Arlo rolled his eyes. "Keep your jackets." He clenched his jaw to stop it from knocking.

The moon lit their way, but as the path dwindled, so did the light. Now and again, Arlo tried shining his flashlight into the forest, but it barely penetrated a few yards. Once or twice he thought he heard footsteps, but when he stopped to listen, all he could hear was another owl hoot and a distant roar of rushing water.

At last, they reached the end of the wood. A low stone wall bisected the path and ran along the forest's edge. Stones piled one on top of the other, forming a barrier.

On the other side of the low wall, the path widened and sloped downhill. The moon, almost full, illuminated the clearing. At the base, there was an old covered bridge that traversed a small river. On the other side was a shallow basin where the town lay bathed in silver.

"Hey," said Lola with an impish grin. "Why do we say it's sunny out, but we never say it's moony?" They all chuckled. But it was a hollow sound, quickly swallowed by silence.

In the twilight, Arlo could see the outline of buildings. He had been expecting something like what they'd passed on their drive, but this town—if you could call it that—was little more than a smattering of old structures on either side of a narrow street. In the distance, he could see the silhouette of a church steeple and a mill, which he recognized by its enormous wheel.

"Welcome to Livermore," said Lola. "Population: us."

Arlo smiled, but something told him she might be right. "Come on," he said, urging them onward. He helped his mother over the low wall and then down the hill. "Let's get help."

The descent into town was difficult. His mother's makeshift cast was starting to sag. She was putting on a brave face, but Arlo could tell she was in pain.

At the base of the hill, the ground leveled. Arlo paused for a moment before entering the old covered bridge. "Are you sure this is safe?" he called out, but his mother and Lola had already crossed the threshold. The floor timbers and wide arches creaked and moaned in protest of their weight.

Inhaling deeply, he detected a slight scent of rot and worried the old planks might give way beneath them. He also questioned how cars managed to cross the narrow rickety lane but quickly decided that between the low wall and the bridge, there must be another road in and out of town.

He took one tentative step, then another. Feeling his weight supported, he caught up to the others, forming a tight group. As they trod forward, the scent of rot grew thicker. It smelled like old wood and something else. Something animal-like.

Arlo was suddenly reminded of the old tale of "The Three Billy Goats Gruff," and for a fleeting moment, he wondered if perhaps there was a nasty troll poised to eat the three of them at the other end. He was immensely relieved to exit the canopy of creaky timber without a troll, a goat, or so much as a chipmunk or field mouse sighting.

Out in the open he got a better view of the town. Livermore wasn't quite as small as it had first appeared. Still, it was little more than a dot on an old road map, a collection of buildings blown together by a strong wind.

Like a black-and-white photo, it had a washed-out quality, as though it had been used up and discarded long ago. It certainly didn't look as though there'd be anything remotely close to a hospital. Their best bet was to get a signal. Or find someone with a landline and a car.

Two-story houses clustered at odd angles along the dirt lane, each with its own covered porch and short picket fence. By design, Arlo figured they had never been rebuilt and were probably nearly a century and a half old. Though they seemed sturdy enough, the white clapboard—more gray in the twilight—had lost more paint than it had kept, giving the structures an air of decay. The wind picked up, funneling between the buildings, making a low, mournful howl.

As they approached the first building, Arlo's senses sharpened and he became acutely aware something wasn't quite right. Despite the early hour, there should have been light—a porch light left on, a streetlamp lit, the iridescent glow of cable boxes, clocks, and digital devices emanating from windows. There should have been sounds—creaking floors, the hum of electronics. Instead the silence was so thick he could taste it.

It was the day before Thanksgiving. People stayed up late or woke up early, preparing food, visiting with friends and relatives, watching TV. But the whole town seemed to be blanketed in darkness. And silence. As if it were slumbering just behind a thin, earthy veil.

"I've been in graveyards more welcoming than this place," said his mother.

"Hey," said Lola. "Why couldn't the skeleton get into the cemetery?" She paused momentarily before blurting out the punch line. "He had nobody to go with! Get it? No *body*?"

Arlo tried to smile, but he wasn't in the mood for any humor, let alone cemetery humor. He felt like an intruder in this strange place. Like he ought to turn around and head back to the main road. But they'd come a long way. He was exhausted and cold, and he could see that the dark spot on the T-shirt wrapped around his mother's ankle had grown.

He summoned his courage, walked up to the first house, and opened the creaky wooden gate. He mounted the porch steps and gave the door a timid knock. He waited, hopeful, but nothing stirred. Not even a curtain twitched.

The frigid air was turning the moisture on Lola's eyelashes into diamonds. Her eyes were pale and shiny, and a silvery spot, like a lacy snowflake, glistened on her cheek. Was it the beginnings of frostbite? They had to find shelter. And quick.

Arlo moved on to the next dwelling and tried it as well. Again, there was no response other than the complaints of the creaky gate and steps.

"Maybe no one lives here," he said. "Maybe this is some kind of ghost town."

"It's early. They're probably sleeping," said his mother. "And it doesn't feel abandoned."

"Look," said Lola.

She pointed to a porch on which sat a clay pot. In it were bright orange mums that had most definitely been planted there. The stems were drooping, but the plant was alive. The night's moisture had covered the blooms in a thin layer of frost.

Arlo looked around. Despite the flowers, the town still felt deserted. He left his mother and sister and crossed the street, opened yet another gate, and approached a third door.

He paused for what felt like an age. And then he made a fist and gave the warped wood a gentle rap. He counted ten seconds. Fifteen. Time seemed to warp along with the wood, curling around him.

It was still dark, but the air had begun to change. The sun, not yet visible, was painting the sky a deep sapphire. Arlo checked his phone—the battery had switched to low-power mode. He attempted to find a signal. Still nothing.

He knocked again, this time harder. There was another long pause. He'd nearly turned from that door as well when suddenly it creaked open.

Twilight transformed the open doorway into the shape of a crooked coffin. A figure stood just beyond it, draped in shadow. From the silhouette, Arlo could tell it was a woman. She was tall and lean and wore a bathrobe cinched tight at the waist.

"What do you want?" she said in a terse, nearly toneless voice.

Arlo's valor drained into his sneakers. A lump swelled in his throat, and he had difficulty navigating his words past it. "M-My mother . . ." he stammered. "She needs help."

The woman leaned forward. Arlo thought he caught sight of pale pig-like eyes staring intently at him. Then the woman craned her neck, peering beyond his shoulder.

"You've come to the wrong place," she said, the words so brittle they threatened to snap.

Arlo's mother tottered up alongside him. "Sorry to trouble you—especially at this hour—but we've had an accident, and we can't seem to get a signal. Could we please use your phone?"

The woman stood statuesque. "Like I said, you've come to the wrong place." She was about to shut the door when Arlo heard a tiny voice chime like fine glass.

"Who is it, Lovicia?"

"Strangers," said the woman. She attempted to shut the door again, but Lola burst forth and jammed it open with her foot.

"We need your help."

Lola was small in stature, but something in her posture, in the determined fierceness of her action, caused the woman to step back and withdraw further into the shadows. Lola had that effect on people.

The woman was joined by a smaller figure, and there was a brief silence in which Arlo had the distinct feeling they were being scrutinized.

"We must help them," said the little girl at last, her words as spindly as spider legs. She leaned in toward the woman and whispered something. Arlo caught fragments that sounded like ". . . nameless . . ." and ". . . awake . . ."

With visible reluctance, Lovicia stepped aside. Before Arlo could voice his concern, Lola traipsed past him, followed by their mother. The cool wind clawed at his back. He knew he had to enter quickly or the desire to turn and bolt would overpower him.

His mother needed help. It was all that mattered. His brain communicated with his legs, instructing them to carry him past the threshold. Lovicia shut the door softly behind him.

For a brief moment, darkness overwhelmed him, sharpening his other senses. The room smelled sour and musty. Footsteps retreated and then quickly returned. He heard the scrape and hiss of a struck match, the flare sending shadows scurrying to the corners of the room.

The little girl stood holding a brass saucer with the stub of a lit candle. She placed it on a long wooden table beside a wicker basket filled with red apples.

In the candlelight Arlo got a good look at his hosts. The little girl wore bright yellow pajamas with red polka dots. Her face was pale, with delicate features flanked by two brown braids, while Lovicia's was narrow and angular with a hook nose and salt-and-pepper hair gathered up into a bird's nest. Shadows buried themselves in the hollows of the woman's cheeks. Her eyes were so sunken you could have dug for treasure in them. Arlo cast his gaze downward and noticed her brittle, yellowing toenails.

The inside of the house—more like a cottage—wasn't altogether ugly. It may have even been what Arlo's mother would describe as *quaint and cozy* were it not as frigid as the outside. He shivered.

"I think we should light a fire, Lovicia," said the girl. "We wouldn't want our guests to catch a chill."

"I'm not cold," said Lola, removing her jacket and depositing it on the wooden bench.

"A fire would be nice," said Arlo's mother, opting to keep hers on.

Lovicia's eyes tapered suspiciously before she turned her back on her guests and headed to the hearth. It was enormous and dominated the space. Arlo had never seen anything quite like it. It was made of red brick with a large wooden mantel displaying pewter dishes and cups of varying size.

While Lovicia arranged logs in the huge opening and struck another match, igniting pinecones and kindling, the girl lit two more candles, and the room came alive with a warm orange glow.

Above the fire hung a pot. Metal spoons and ladles

dangled from hooks. To the right of the large opening were two smaller openings, one on top of the other. The bottom contained more logs, while the top appeared to be a sort of oven.

Beside the fireplace was a wooden contraption resembling a butter churn. On the other side was a broom made entirely of sticks. Bunches of herbs bound with string hung drying from the mantel. It all reminded Arlo of an illustration in a book of fairy tales by the brothers Grimm.

"Please," said the girl. "Have a seat." She motioned to the benches alongside the table.

Though he was still shivering, Arlo scuttled as far from the fire as possible. Lola sat beside him, and his mother plunked herself down opposite them, setting the crutch on the floor and hoisting her leg onto the bench.

"I'm Hannah." In the firelight the girl's cheeks took on a rosy hue. Her hair appeared lighter than Arlo had first imagined—the color of hazelnuts. In the darkness she had appeared pale and homely. In the glow of the embers, she was kind of cute—in that little-kid-in-a-candy-commercial way.

"This is Lovicia." She motioned toward the woman and smiled. "My *very old* aunt."

Lovicia scowled at Hannah and then nodded a curt greeting.

Not a very nice old aunt, thought Arlo. Not at all like his aunt Anita, who tossed the football with him and braided Lola's hair and let them stay up late watching old movies.

Arlo's mother extended her hand. It dangled like an unanswered question, so the shake became a wave. "Heather Flores. Pleased to meet you."

"I'm Lola, and this is Arlo. He hates fire. It scares him. It's why he won't go camping. Or even roast marshmallows, or . . ."

Arlo glowered. "I'm not scared. Just cautious."

"You're scared of everything," she jeered. "You once got scared of a chipmunk."

"I thought it had rabies!" He gave her a sharp kick under the table.

"Hey!" Lola shouted.

Arlo's mother groaned. At first, he thought it was meant to scold them for their bickering, but then he saw her reach for her ankle. He scooched closer to her so that he was sitting directly opposite.

"I need a doctor," she said softly. "Is there a hospital nearby?"

Lovicia stared at Hannah. A silent message seemed to pass between them.

"I'll fetch Doc Brown," said Hannah. "I'm sure he can fix you up in no time."

"A hospital would be better," said Arlo. "Could you drive us? Or call an ambulance?"

"We don't have a telephone," said Hannah. "And no car. No one round here does."

Arlo's mother's face fell. "No phone?"

"Not even a cell?" said Lola. She looked bewildered.

"Not much use for either," said Lovicia.

"But . . ." protested Lola. "No *phone*?" The idea was like an unchewed meatball she had trouble swallowing.

"How do you get around?" said Arlo.

"We lead a simple life. No need for complications," said Lovicia sharply. She added more kindling to the fire, poking harshly at the logs with a large iron fork. "We keep to ourselves." She eyed Arlo in way that might indicate, *Which is what I suggest you do.*

"We must seem strange," said Hannah.

No phone. No car. Strange didn't even begin to describe it. Arlo suddenly felt like he was on a reality TV show. One of those shows where the producers make the participants live without modern technology so they can amuse audiences with their struggles. *Survivor:*

Livermore. He scanned the room, searching for a hidden camera. It almost made him smile, but then his mother moaned again.

"Dr. Brown would be great," she said, rubbing her leg.

Hannah nodded. She moved toward the window. The sun was beginning to color the air. "I'll get dressed and fetch him." She turned on her heels and marched up a narrow staircase at the far end of the room. "Do make our guests comfortable, Aunt Lovicia," she called over her shoulder.

Arlo got up and stood beside his mother. He hovered over her, wondering what he could do to help. "You sure you're going to be okay?"

She nodded. "Of course."

Arlo gazed at her doubtfully. "Maybe we should try and get to a farmhouse along the main road?"

"Let's wait and see what the doctor says. You did a great job, Arlo, but I don't think I can walk any more without a proper cast."

Hannah returned quickly, wearing a pair of jeans with patches at the knees and a gray sweatshirt three sizes too big. She pulled on leather boots and laced them. Taking a green wool jacket from a hook, she swung it over her tiny shoulders.

"I'll be back in a wink," she said cheerfully. "Have

something to eat. You must be famished." She slipped out the door and shut it behind her.

Lola picked up a large apple, then seemed to think twice about it, returning it to the basket. "Have you got anything else?"

Lovicia walked toward a shelf, opened a large wooden box, and retrieved a brownish hunk. She placed it on the counter and began slicing it with a large knife.

Leaning in close to his mother, Arlo whispered, "This is weird. I say we leave. I'll help you . . ."

"Don't be silly," said his mother under her breath. "Maybe they don't believe in technology. Nothing wrong with that. I kind of like it, it's . . ."

"Quaint and cozy?" offered Arlo.

His mother grinned. "Just like that community in upstate New York where Grandma Pearl buys baked goods, crafts, and smoked bacon from animals raised without antibiotics or hormones . . ."

Arlo gazed around at the room. He'd seen loads of programs about remote communities that shunned modern conveniences and functioned quite well without them. Maybe his mother was right. Maybe he was being overly suspicious.

Lovicia advanced in a stately manner and deposited

a plate of brown bread, some butter, cheese, a jar of preserves, and one with honey on the table. She turned, retrieved a dull knife from a pantry drawer, and placed that on the table as well.

"Blueberry?" said Lola, holding the jar of preserves. "I love blueberry."

"Huckleberry," said Lovicia crisply. "Now, if you'll excuse me." She turned and disappeared up the stairs.

Arlo eyed the items on the table. None looked like they'd come from a store. He was used to his mother's packaged and processed foods. She'd never make her own jam, let alone bread.

He watched his mother take a thick slice and smother it in jam. She ate heartily. Arlo stood, backed away from the table, and wandered toward the window.

The glass was filmy, but he could see out well enough. Pale November sunlight leaked over the horizon as dawn heralded the new day.

"It doesn't taste very sweet . . ." complained Lola.

"Tastes fine to me . . ."

While the two ate and argued, Arlo contemplated the scenery. The town of Livermore wasn't quite so dreary anymore. He was amazed at how, with a little light, it could almost pass as cheerful.

He'd flattened his cheek against the cold glass to search for any sign of Hannah when over his shoulder he heard a low voice.

"Leave now. While you still can."

Each word was bitten off so that the ends were sharp and jagged, their sound snagging in his ears.

Arlo swung round.

Lovicia stood inches from him, her long nose practically touching his, her lips a thin, hard line. He could smell her breath, pungent as cooked cabbage. Despite her stooping to his level, she seemed far more imposing than previously.

Before Arlo could react, the door burst open and Lovicia stepped back. Her fierce expression melted into a cool complacency. Hannah had returned with a small man Arlo could only assume was Doc Brown.

Arlo's mother set down her jam sandwich—apparently oblivious to Arlo's interaction with Lovicia. "You must be Dr. Brown. I'm sure glad to meet you."

The doctor wore a black coat, a tweed vest, and a bow tie. Everything about him—the scuffed brown shoes, the black medical bag, the lank hair, gray beard, and mustache—had a crumpled, worn quality. His age was uncertain, but Arlo thought he looked ancient. He had a gloomy expression, as though all light and joy had been surgically removed from his soul.

"Nehemiah Brown. Pleased to make your acquaintance," he said cordially. "Though I suppose the circumstances are not what one would call pleasant." He glanced at Arlo, then at Lola, his milky white eyes still sharp and keen.

"You can say that again," said Arlo's mother, attempting to sit up straighter. She winced and shrunk back down. "As you can see, I've got a bit of a situation."

"I'm certain it's nothing we can't handle," said the doctor. He pushed the basket of apples aside and set his black leather bag on the table. "Lovicia, boil some water."

Lovicia nodded stiffly. She retreated, taking a copper kettle from the mantel, ladled water from a large wooden bucket beside the sink into it, and then hung it over the fire, replacing the pot.

"Hannah has told me you've had some sort of accident."

Hannah nodded. "Yes—though, I completely forgot to ask what happened."

"We hit a moose," said Arlo. "Then a tree."

"With our car," added Lola as if to avoid any confusion.

"Oh," said Hannah. "I hope it's okay."

There was enough ambiguity in her tone to make Arlo wonder if she'd meant the car, the moose, or the tree.

Sunlight flowed through the window and extended merrily over the table toward the fireplace. Hannah blew out the candles, their light no longer necessary, sending thin coils of smoke curling into air.

Arlo inhaled deeply. He'd always loved the ashy scent of snuffed-out candles. It reminded him of birthday cake. He often thought they should make a candle that smelled like blown-out candles.

Doc Brown knelt by Arlo's mother's side and began gingerly unraveling the strips of torn T-shirt and removing the sticks from the makeshift cast. "It's not too often we get visitors. And hardly ever this late in the season . . ."

"Sometimes hikers and hunters get lost and need directions," said Hannah. "Sometimes they even stay a night. Never longer . . ."

Arlo's mother flinched. He could tell the pain was sharper, more urgent. He wanted to dive toward her and rescue her—not let this stranger touch her—but instead he turned toward the window. The final cloth was being removed. He didn't know if he could handle seeing the open wound again. The first time it made him sick, and that was under the influence of all that adrenaline. This time he just might pass out.

"Ugh!" said Lola. "That's disgusting!"

"I'm sure it looks worse than it is, right, Doc?" said Arlo's mother.

"It's not good. I'll say that much. I'm going to have to clean the wound and set the bone. Lovicia, I'll need your strength. The muscles have contracted, and we'll need to stretch them to get the bone in the right place. It's going to smart quite a bit. I can give you a whiff of ether, if you like."

"I'd prefer a martini," said Arlo's mother, but no one laughed.

Out of the corner of his eye, Arlo watched the man withdraw a few items from his bag, including a spool of black thread, a long needle, a wooden splint, some white cloth, and a vial of colorless liquid.

"Hannah," he said, "why don't you show these children around town whilst I get this matter settled." The girl nodded brightly.

"No," said Arlo firmly, lunging for his mother. He

wouldn't abandon her—especially not to the nasty Lovicia and the grim doctor.

"Dr. Brown is right. It's best you and Lola don't see this."

Arlo glanced at the gaping wound and felt his knees grow weak.

"It'll make it easier for your mother if she doesn't have to conceal her pain for your sake, son," said the man.

Arlo sighed. The last thing he wanted to do was make things harder for his mother. He looked her in the eye. They shared a type of telepathy. She knew what he was thinking.

"Go on." She nodded.

Arlo's thoughts tunneled back through time. He recalled the plump, chirpy nurse with the mop of blond hair who had registered his mother, recorded her height and weight, and taken her pulse, blood pressure, and temperature before inserting an IV. His mother had received something to prevent nausea and allergic reactions and then the sitting had begun.

It's going to be okay.

Above the fire, the kettle began to wheeze and whistle.

"Come on. Let's go," said Lola, grabbing Arlo's jacket. "Let's check out the town."

"Okay," he said, uprooting his feet. "We won't go far." He only managed the last words before Lola dragged him out the door.

The air inside the house had been sufficiently heated by the fireplace, making the outside feel all the chillier. Arlo's breath plumed around him as he followed the girls along the dirt road. Lola sidled jovially alongside Hannah, who chatted to her as though they had been best friends forever.

"I'm so glad you came," she said cheerfully. "New blood . . ."

"My blood isn't new. It's almost nine years old," said Lola.

Hannah laughed. "What I mean is, I like meeting new people. I get so tired of the same old faces, day after day. Hardly anybody new ever comes around here—especially no one young. It's so dull and dreary."

Arlo glanced around. In the daylight, Livermore was less forbidding. How could it have been so intimidating a few hours ago? Now it looked almost pitiful.

The main road sloped upward past several small homes, each similar to Lovicia's and none more inviting.

Arlo counted eleven homes in total. Seven on one side of the street, four on the other.

A muscular-looking man with dark skin, dressed in black pants with suspenders, a white button-down shirt with the sleeves rolled up, and a black felt hat, stood sweeping his porch in front of one of these houses. It was one that Arlo had knocked on earlier and had received no response.

"Morning, Simon," said Hannah cheerfully.

The man stopped sweeping. He seemed surprised to see them. Then he narrowed his eyes, touched the brim of his hat, nodded, and grumbled, "Morning."

"That's Simon Sandborn," whispered Hannah. "He's forever grumpy."

The man held his broom in one hand and observed them warily. Arlo could feel the man's curious gaze linger on his back long after they'd passed.

Beyond the homes that neatly lined the dirt road were a smattering of other houses here and there in the hillside. As the road sloped upward, they neared the top of the hill where sat a single immense dwelling. It cast a long shadow over the street. In the early morning darkness, they had missed it entirely.

The side view was already impressive, but as they

approached the front, Arlo drew in his breath. The house was massive by any standard, but by Livermore standards, it was a veritable mansion. Set atop a hill that sloped down to the river on one side, with mountain peaks rising off in the distance, it was an imposing sight.

The structure had countless gables, two chimneys, and two hexagonal rooms that rose higher than the rest, with small turreted roofs. A rusty weathervane creaked from the pinnacle, as it spun in the breeze.

The wood siding was dark, but picket fences and ornate wood trim had retained more white paint than any of the other homes, giving the mansion a further air of luxury. It was two stories across the front, but as it was built on the hillside, it had another floor below that was visible from the side. There was a large porch in front of the house and enormous terraces on either side with balconies above on the second floor.

"What is this?" asked Arlo.

"The Samuels Mansion," said Hannah matter-of-factly. "They own the mill. And the town."

"I want to own a town," said Lola. "I'd call it Lolaville. There would be ten dog parks, five ice cream parlors, a roller coaster for transportation, definitely no schools, and . . ."

Arlo ignored his sister's ramblings. All those

gables made him think of a witch house in Salem, Massachusetts, he'd seen in a pop-up ad—a creepy but popular tourist attraction.

"Arlo," said Lola, thumping him on the shoulder. "Are you even listening?"

Arlo snapped from his trance.

"Hannah said it's a bed-and-breakfast. Just like the one we were supposed to stay at," said Lola.

He nodded absentmindedly, still studying the sloping roof, the acute angles of the gables, and the draped windows. He was about to turn away when one of the curtains lifted and a pale face framed with brown hair appeared.

Hannah sprang forward, waving excitedly. "Alice!"

The figure retreated, and the curtain flopped shut.

"That's Alice Samuels," said Hannah. "She's shy. Doesn't like strangers. Most people here don't. But I do. I love new people. Come on . . ." She took Lola's hand. "I'll show you the rest of town."

Past the mansion, a line of railroad tracks crossed the main street. There were no bars or barriers, just the old ties set into the gravel and rocks with rusty spikes and rustier rails overtop. To the left, the tracks split, one set heading toward a rickety building.

"That's the depot," said Hannah. "And there's the

old brick engine house. That's the grocery store, and what used to be a blacksmith, and the post office . . ."

Arlo looked right, then left before setting foot onto the tracks. He imagined he heard a hollow whistle echo in the distance. He stuck a finger to his ear, but the ringing stopped.

"Oh, don't worry." Hannah chuckled. She stopped smack-dab in the middle of the tracks and stretched her arms wide. "Old Peggy hasn't run in ages."

"Old Peggy?" asked Lola. "Is that a friend of yours?"

"Peggy was the old locomotive of the line. We had a heavy flood. Parts of the railroad bed and the bridges were damaged. Then the mill shut down and, along with it, the railroad. Old Peggy's been retired for some time." She pointed left, beyond the depot. "That's the mill."

Arlo could see the enormous wheel—the same one he'd seen from the other side of the river. There was a pond with piles of old logs lying along its banks.

"This way," said Hannah, pulling on Lola's sleeve. "I'll show you the school."

A crisp wind scattered leaves and debris. Hannah's wool jacket flapped as she scampered up the street with Lola at her side. Neither seemed affected by the cold.

They passed a little Episcopal church—a modest building with a spire that could barely graze a cloud, let alone pierce the heavens—and another building Hannah explained was St. George's Hall. Writhing twists of ivy choked its walls, holding the brick and mortar together like Scotch tape.

"This is where folks used to get their hunting and fishing licenses," said Hannah. She looked at the building solemnly. "But that's all done in the towns these days."

The group stopped in front of a small structure with a steep roof and a flagpole complete with a slightly tattered flag flapping in the breeze. It had four large windows on either side.

"There's no school today," said Hannah. "Or I'd show you the inside."

"Oh, don't worry," said Lola. "I hate school. Except recess. I love recess."

"It was voted *best school in the state* one year," said Hannah proudly. "Very progressive. Of course, that was a long time ago . . ."

Arlo contemplated the shabby building. He figured the school couldn't hold more than a single classroom. He'd never seen anything like it except in pioneer films. *Progressive* wasn't a word that came to mind.

"Any other interesting things to see?" asked Lola.

"Well . . . there's a library further up the street. We

have hundreds of books. Have you read *Robinson Crusoe*?"

Lola frowned. Arlo shook his head.

"Never mind, then," she sighed. "There's not much past the library. Just Doc Brown's house. And the grave-yard. I suppose you don't want to see those?"

Arlo squinted. He could see a flat expanse of land cordoned off with a short, tilting wrought-iron fence. Gray tombstones sprang from wild grass and weeds, slanting at odd angles.

"I'm afraid that's pretty much the whole town," said Hannah. "Except for Little Canada over on the other side of the river."

Arlo might have asked what Little Canada was but his mind got stuck on the words *doctor* and *graveyard*. A pang of worry speared his chest. How long had they been gone? It couldn't have been more than a half hour, but it felt like forever. Instinctively, he withdrew his phone from his pocket and powered it up to check the time.

"We should head back," he said.

As they retraced their steps, past the old structures—their wood freckled with dry rot—past the mill and the abandoned railroad, a thought came swiftly to Arlo. The town of Livermore was a desolate and forgotten place. But perhaps it had been left behind for good reason.

Halfway back, at the top of the hill in front of the Samuels Mansion, he realized he was still holding his phone. He was about to tuck it into his pocket, when he noticed he had a signal.

6

"**D**ad! Hey, Dad!"

Arlo had been so shocked to see the signal he'd speed-dialed the first person on his list—his father. His battery was only twelve percent. He had to talk quickly.

"Listen, Dad! We had an accident!"

"What did you say? You're breaking up."

"An ac-ci-dent!" shouted Lola. She sprang to Arlo's side and had her ear to the phone as well.

"The car's a wreck. It's not drivable," said Arlo.

Arlo's father seemed equal parts upset and annoyed. "An accident! Are you okay? Are you injured? Where's your mother?"

"I'm fine," said Arlo.

"I'm fine, too!" said Lola.

"Mom broke her ankle, though," said Arlo. "It's not good—even the doctor—"

There was some crackling on the line. ". . . she's with a doctor? That's good. Where are you?"

"A place called Livermore. Can you come get us?"

More crackling. Arlo was afraid the call would drop. ". . . Thanksgiving . . . turkey in oven . . . Reginald . . . sniffles . . . Renée's family . . ."

Arlo exchanged glances with Lola. They could fill in the blanks easily enough. Lola was less forgiving, but Arlo knew his father was busy. He had responsibilities.

Arlo looked down at his phone. Ten percent. "Dad! I don't have much battery. Can you just come get us? Please?" He turned away from Hannah and whispered, "This place is weird."

"Sure. Of course. I'll come get you tomorrow," his father said. "Is there a motel?"

Arlo thought of the Samuelses' house. The bed-and-breakfast. "Yes . . . but . . ."

"Stay the night . . . I'll come tomorrow. Livermore, you said? I'll look it up."

"But, Dad!"

"Look, Arlo . . ."

His father launched into a brief monologue that cut in and out, but Arlo got the gist. Of course, his father couldn't just drop everything and run off. He had plans, too. They were to either call his aunt Anita or wait for him. Tomorrow was the best he could do. If he and Lola were okay, his mother's broken ankle wasn't too bad—especially if she was being tended to by a doctor. Tomorrow afternoon. Or early evening. He'd be there. He promised. Arlo could count on him.

He finished off with, "How will I find you once I'm there?"

Arlo glanced around at the scant homes and buildings. "Trust me—it won't be hard." His battery had fallen to eight percent. He had to power down if he hoped to get in one more call. "If I can reach Aunt Anita, I'll let you know."

"Liver . . . more?"

"Yup. See you tomorrow." Arlo powered down quickly, hoping to conserve the final remnants of battery life. He couldn't waste even a minute on a useless call. Before he tried Aunt Anita, he'd check in with his mother and see what she thought.

"I do hope it snows soon," Hannah was saying cheerfully. She pointed down the slope toward her house. "We sled down this hill. It's so much fun."

"Cool," said Lola. "Let it snow! Snow! Snow!" She

turned in a circle, doing an improvised rain—or, in this case, snow—dance.

Arlo sped past her the remainder of the way back to Lovicia's. He was elated and frustrated and relieved and worried, and all these emotions boiled and bubbled in his stomach, making him slightly queasy. He burst into the door without knocking and was thrilled to see his mother sitting up, all alone, her leg properly bandaged with a splint. A musky scent filled the air. She had a teacup to her lips.

"Hey!" she said, as though she hadn't a care in the world. "Have fun checking out the sights?"

Lola and Hannah entered the house giggling.

"I got a signal," said Arlo breathlessly. He plunked himself beside her. "I called Dad."

"Great!"

"He's coming to get us," said Arlo.

"Really?" said his mother. "On Thanksgiving? That's pretty impressive."

"Well." Arlo swallowed. "He *is* coming . . . but not today. Tomorrow. Afternoon. Or early evening."

Her smile quivered slightly. "Tomorrow. Okay. Perfect."

Arlo could tell what she was thinking. "There's a mansion up the hill," he said quickly.

"And guess what?" added Lola. "It's a bed-and-breakfast. Just like we were going to stay at. Probably even nicer."

"Really?" She perked up. "A mansion? Maybe they have a room?"

"It's huge," said Lola.

"It's really impressive. Like something out of an old movie." Arlo glanced at her cast. It looked nothing like the plastic air cast his friend Wesley had worn after rolling his ankle playing basketball last year, but it appeared solid and clean, and he supposed that was all that mattered.

"Can you walk?" he asked.

"As soon as the starch concoction Doc put on the cloth hardens. In fact, he recommends it. Says *exercise is important to prevent muscle atrophy during immobilization . . .*" She used an exaggerated haughty air that made them both chuckle.

Her laugh morphed into a throat clearing, however, when the doctor reentered from a back room with Lovicia by his side. Both wore matching grim expressions.

"Is she going to be all right?" asked Arlo, worry creeping back into his tone.

"Fine," said the doctor. "Just fine. The wound is clean

and closed. No sign of infection. The bone set in place nicely. You did a good job protecting it, young man. It should be good as new in a month or two."

Worry dissipated as Arlo's chest swelled with pride.

"They're going to stay at the Samuelses' place," said Hannah.

"No," said Lovicia flatly.

Everyone stopped and stared at her.

Lovicia's face remained even and expressionless, but her voice softened. "It's best they leave now. In the daylight. As soon as the cast has set."

"Oh, Aunt Lovicia, you know they can't go now," said Hannah, taking Lola's hand and swinging it as if to flaunt her new friendship. "Their father will be coming for them tomorrow. And besides, it's Thanksgiving. Have you forgotten about the celebration?"

"The celebration," said Lovicia vaguely, as though her thoughts were eons away. She and the doctor exchanged glances.

"Yes!" Hannah beamed. "It's a Thanksgiving tradition. The Samuelses have a harvest dinner each year at the mansion. There will be music and dancing. The entire town attends."

"Well," said the doctor, "I'm heading past the Samuelses' house now. I'll check with Woodbridge—see if he can't give them a room no charge, what with the accident and all."

"Oh, gosh," said Arlo's mother. "I hadn't even thought about money. My purse is in the car."

"Woodbridge Samuels is an understanding fellow," said the doctor. "I'll make sure he has a room ready."

Was it Arlo's imagination, or had the doctor's gaze found Lovicia's once more?

Lovicia nodded and took a wicker basket that hung from a hook on the ceiling. "I'd best begin preparations. We all help with the meal. And we eat early around here." She wrapped a woolen cloak around her shoulders and left alongside the doctor.

Arlo had forgotten all about Thanksgiving until his father had mentioned it. He didn't recall seeing anything remotely close to a town celebration underway. No pumpkins. No cornucopias. Definitely no giant inflatable turkeys. He sighed.

All the talk of Thanksgiving and celebrations made Arlo suddenly and acutely aware he hadn't eaten anything since the bite of Little Debbie cake. His stomach growled ferociously. His mother tossed him one of the ripe red apples from the basket on the table. He bobbled it and then secured the catch. He took a large bite and found it surprisingly fresh and sweet and juicy.

"Are you all right?" his mother asked, reaching over and gently touching a bruise on his cheek. "You don't look good."

"I'm fine," said Arlo, brushing her hand away. His mother frowned. "Really. Don't worry."

They stayed awhile in the small house. With the help of the heat emanating from fireplace, the cast set. His mother had more tea while Arlo had some jam and bread. Lola and Hannah disappeared for some time up the narrow stairs. When they returned, they were wearing old-fashioned dresses.

Lola whirled round. "What do you think?"

Arlo's jaw dropped. "Where are your overalls?"

"Upstairs." She twirled again.

"But . . ." said Arlo, "you hate dresses."

"Gorgeous!" said his mother, waving a dismissive hand at Arlo as though he were a pesky fly. "Not sure about the soccer cleats, though . . ." She chuckled.

"Isn't it a bit cold for dresses?" muttered Arlo, but no one responded.

"Ready?" asked Hannah. "We should get you to the Samuelses' place now. Like Lovicia told you. It's an early celebration. You could stay here . . ." She seemed to ponder as she spoke. "But there isn't a lot of space. You'd be far more comfortable in your own room."

Arlo helped his mother to her feet. The cast seemed solid enough—a far cry from the sagging monstrosity he'd created. Now that it had hardened somewhat, it looked just like the casts he was used to seeing.

Arlo's mother emptied what remained of their drive snacks onto the table and wrapped the plastic bag around her foot to keep the cast clean. The branch she'd used as a crutch worked even better since she could put some weight on her foot. Still, the stroll uphill to the Samuels Mansion wasn't exactly a breeze.

"Wow." His mother whistled, getting the full view of the house as they stood in front. "Do you know what this reminds me of?"

"A Salem witch house," muttered Arlo.

"No," she shook her head. "More like that haunted mansion in San Jose."

Arlo gulped. He wasn't sure which image he liked less.

There were two entrances to the enormous home. Hannah had gone ahead to the one located at the center of the house and knocked on the door. Beyond the panes of frosted glass there was nothing but darkness. The porch had a forlorn appearance, the corners clotted with crusted leaves and debris.

Arlo spied something shifting in the hall's black depths. There was movement and then a pale light blossomed. Someone was approaching. He was expecting the girl, Alice, but when the door creaked open, a man appeared.

He was a middle-aged gentleman in a black suit with shiny black shoes and a black bowler hat. A large handlebar mustache was the focal point of his gaunt, angular face. He didn't look like a woodsman or mill owner at all. Minus the hat and mustache, he seemed more like a preacher.

"Ah," he said in a pleasant but stiff tone. "You must be the guests Doc Brown spoke of."

"Hi, Mr. Samuels," chirped Hannah.

He tipped his hat formally and held the door wide as she and Lola stepped inside.

"Fancy," whispered Arlo's mother.

"Yeah," he replied, trying to sound as cheerful as she, though his smile flickered and vanished, leaving unease in its place.

As Arlo crossed the threshold, his eyes locked momentarily with the man's. Mr. Samuels smiled beneath his mammoth mustache, but there was no warmth or kindliness in his face. It was a foxlike expression, eyes crinkled and cunning, a smile hiding sharp teeth.

The splendor of the home's exterior was eclipsed only by its interior. As they stood in the large foyer, Arlo was immediately overwhelmed by the high ceilings and faded grandeur. Impossible not to see first was the enormous staircase that stretched into the shadows of the second story.

As his eyes adjusted to the dim light, he noticed more details. Polished wooden floors matched the ornate wooden trim that rose halfway up the walls. The other half was covered in a faded-green paisley-patterned paper with splotches where moths must have eaten away at it. Arlo had once read that Victorian green wallpaper contained arsenic that actually killed people. He made note to stand clear of the murderous walls. Just in case.

Flames flickered behind glass shades on large sconces that hung at intervals. Oily lamplight oozed down the walls and puddled on the ground at Arlo's feet.

At either side of the foyer were archways leading to hallways that disappeared into voids of darkness. Heavy floor-length drapes patterned with parrots and palms framed the windows, letting in little natural light. The air was stagnant and dense and smelled faintly of lavender. Dust motes sparkled where they managed to catch the light, giving the air a strange, almost magical feel.

"Welcome," said Woodbridge Samuels. "We're happy to have you stay the night and join our celebration." He grinned at Hannah.

"I, well," Arlo's mother stammered. "I can't pay you right now. But I can give you my credit card number or send you an etransfer once I'm home."

"Not to worry," said Woodbridge, pulling a cord on the wall. A bell chimed. "Doc Brown explained your predicament. I'm sure we can come to an arrangement."

A woman entered through the right hallway. She was

short and stout with a stern, sullen face. She wore a long black skirt and a crisp white shirt with an apron overtop. Her hair was fixed in a tight bun at the back of her head. Her gaze swept their rumpled clothes and the cast before settling on their faces.

"This is Mrs. Hawthorn. She will see you to your rooms and then bring you lunch," he said.

"Rooms?" Arlo swallowed. "As in more than one?"

"Our rooms aren't terribly large," said Woodbridge Samuels. "We have none that accommodate three."

Arlo stiffened. His mother would stay with Lola for sure. He'd be on his own. "I think we should all stay together," he suggested.

Mrs. Hawthorn regarded him with an unchanging stare. "Now, now. We can't have you sleeping on the floor," she said firmly. "It wouldn't be proper." Something about the way she said it made Arlo think there was no arguing with this woman.

"I'd best get back and help Lovicia," said Hannah, giving Lola's hand a squeeze. "I'll see you at the celebration."

Mrs. Hawthorn gave Hannah a cold stare before turning sharply and leading the way upstairs. A ring of keys jingled in her hand. At the top, she veered left.

"This way," she said. She passed several closed doors

before halting in front of one at the far end of the dark hallway. She flipped through the keys, locating the one she wanted, unlocking the door, and swinging it open into gaping darkness.

She fumbled a moment, then struck a match and lit a pair of sconces on the inside, revealing a lovely room with floral-papered walls and a large brass-framed bed complete with a thick, feathery duvet. There was a wardrobe, a small chest of drawers, and a nightstand with a porcelain pitcher and bowl set on top and a small mirror hanging above. Beneath the curtained window was a small round table with two wooden chairs, and facing the bed was a small fireplace. She marched across the room and yanked open the drapes, letting in the light.

"It's perfect," said Arlo's mother.

"Cool!" said Lola.

As Arlo suspected, he was the odd man out. Sensing his feelings, his mother asked, "Do you have a cot or an inflatable mattress so Arlo can stay with us?"

"I'm afraid not," said Mrs. Hawthorn. "And the wooden floor wouldn't be comfortable."

Arlo didn't want to cause trouble—especially for his mother, who really seemed to like the place. "Don't worry," he said quickly. "Might actually be nice to have my own space for a change."

Mrs. Hawthorn nodded. It was settled. "Bathroom's down the hall. You'll find soap and fresh towels for your convenience there." She turned toward Arlo. "This way."

Arlo was immensely relieved to be hearing the word *bathroom* and not *outhouse*. He had been starting to worry about the plumbing situation.

"All right. If you're okay with it. Then we'll see you in a bit?" said his mother. She lay down on the bed and sunk into the thick duvet.

Arlo followed Mrs. Hawthorn down the hall, past the stairs, to the other wing of the house. They left behind several closed doors Arlo could only assume were other bedrooms or bathrooms before stopping in front of one at the far end.

Mrs. Hawthorn unlocked it and lit the sconces. The room was quite similar to the one his mother and Lola were in, except the bed was smaller, the wallpaper was a different color, and there was only one chair at the round table to the right of the window. She opened the drapes.

"Perfect," he said, echoing his mother's word, though with far less enthusiasm.

He removed his jacket, and his eye caught the small mirror over the nightstand. His ghost stared back.

For the first time since the accident, he took stock of himself. The transformation was startling. His hair was matted, his eyes sunken and hollow. There was a scab in the corner of his mouth and a purple bruise on his right cheek. He touched it and flinched. It was as tender as those on his arm and leg. There was dirt on his chin and beneath his nails, and he had the sudden urge to wash up.

Arlo stepped out into the now empty hall. He couldn't recall which door was the bathroom. He decided to try each, beginning with the one next to his. It was locked, so he moved on. The next was locked as well. When he reached the third, it opened easily, only it wasn't the bathroom. It was another bedroom, and in it stood a girl.

"I—I'm s-sorry," he stammered. "I thought this was the bathroom." He was about to close the door when the girl spoke.

"I saw you earlier."

In the pale glow of the sconces, he got a better look at her. Alice Samuels was tall but slight with a bird-like, angular form. It was likely she weighed less than Lola, though she was significantly taller. She had a small upturned nose, pale skin with a smattering of freckles, and hair—neither yellow nor brown—which hung limp along the sides of her face. She wore a light blue cotton dress similar to those worn by Lola and Hannah, and her hands were buried deep in the sagging pockets of a gray woolen cardigan.

He fanned his fingers. "I'm Arlo."

"Yes," she said, as though she'd already known this. "My father says you are staying the night." She regarded Arlo with hooded eyes that seemed filled with both intrigue and distrust. "I suppose I'll be seeing you at dinner."

He tried to smile, but it was awkward and crooked, and he was suddenly aware he hadn't brushed his teeth in some time. "Okay. Well. See you then."

He shut the door quickly, but quietly, and tried several more doors until he located the bathroom. It was larger than he'd expected, with a great deal of elaborate woodwork. There was a small sink, a tub, and a toilet. A white towel hung on a hook next to the sink. He turned on the faucet, dampened a corner of the towel, and scrubbed his face and teeth. Feeling slightly fresher, he headed over to join his mother and Lola.

As Arlo walked along the hallway, he noticed oil paintings hung here and there—a landscape, a vase with flowers, and a bowl of fruit. There was also a faded photograph—an austere black-and-white portrait of a girl dressed in old-fashioned clothes. Something about it bothered him, like a word on the tip of his tongue he couldn't quite spit out.

He found his mother and Lola relaxing in their room, and the three were soon greeted once again by the dour Mrs. Hawthorn, who brought with her a platter of bread, cheese, and fruit. She also brought two crisp cotton nightgowns and two bathrobes and laid them out on the bed before retreating into the hallway. With nothing else to occupy their time, they ate leisurely.

"I need to rest," said Arlo's mother, yawning and stretching. "I'm beyond exhausted. We've been up for a day and half now."

Lola flopped on the bed. "I feel like I could sleep forever."

"I guess I'll be in my room," said Arlo, "in case you need me."

He was drained as well, and feeling a bit more comfortable in his new surroundings, he thought it best he take a nap. He returned to his room and bounced onto the bed. The mattress was a jungle of coils and lumps, and each time he moved, the metal frame creaked and complained.

He tried for some time to get comfortable but finally gave up and decided to explore the house instead. He slipped out of his room and made his way along the hall and down the stairs.

The Samuels Mansion was a curious sort of place. From the outside, it appeared massive and sprawling, but inside, it was a wilderness of narrow hallways, small rooms, mysterious doors, and little niches all filled with what seemed expensive items—antique vases, candle holders, mirrors, and other knickknacks.

It was strangely quiet as Arlo wandered about the maze of corridors, poking his head into one room, then another. He counted multiple fireplaces, an enormous pipe organ, ornate rugs, and all sorts of interesting chairs. Rooms led into other rooms, and he was almost certain the hallway had doubled back on itself. He was about to turn a corner when he heard a tangle of voices.

Arlo suddenly had the feeling his impromptu tour would not be welcome, so in a spurt of adrenaline, he grabbed for the handle of the nearest door and turned it. He slipped into the darkness of a small, stuffy room and hid in the shadows. By the looks of it, the room was some sort of study, plainly not used in some time.

An enormous desk sat in the center, dust mounding on top of the blotter. Floor-to-ceiling wood shelves rose high and looming, each crammed with ranks of leather-bound books sheathed in cobwebs. Hushed voices echoed in through the open door.

"I'm certain . . ."

"We can't tell yet . . ."

"What shall we do with the other two?"

"Only thing we can do . . ."

"No. It will sort itself out."

"One way . . ."

"Or another . . ."

"If it's true, this must mean . . ."

"It's awake."

"Think of what it might do . . ."

". . . Or undo . . ."

There was a pause in which Arlo heard a collective sigh. Then someone spoke up.

"A gathering might be in order."

"We haven't had a gathering in a dog's age . . ."

"Yes. A gathering. To decide . . ."

"Speaking of gatherings, you will have to excuse me. I have a *harvest dinner* to prepare."

Arlo thought he could make out some of the voices. One was Mr. Samuels. The other, Doc Brown. Certainly, there was Mrs. Hawthorn—or was it perhaps Lovicia? They sounded similar. Another voice was high and shrill. It wasn't Hannah or Alice. He was sure he hadn't heard that one before.

What had they been talking about? What would sort itself out? And who were *the other two*? And what had awakened? No matter which way he spun the conversation, it didn't sound encouraging, but one thing was certain—they were talking about him, his mother, and Lola.

He held his breath a moment, not moving a single muscle until footsteps disappeared down the hallway and he was confident they had all gone. Stepping out of the shadows, he took a deep breath. The room smelled faintly of cigar smoke and strong liquor, mingling with the woody, earthy scent of old paper. Running his hand along a row of leather-bound books, hoping something useful might leap out at him, he randomly plucked one out.

Gold lettering announced *Faust, a Tragedy*, by Johann Wolfgang von Goethe. "Interesting," he said in a mocking tone. He pulled out several other books, including a copy of *Pride and Prejudice*, by Jane Austen; *Wuthering Heights*, by Emily Brontë, and finally *Dracula*, by Bram Stoker.

"A little light reading." He chuckled to himself. He replaced the books and headed deeper into the dark space.

On top of the desk blotter, next to a large inkwell and

quill, sat a different sort of book, blanketed in dust. It was much larger but fairly thin compared to the others. It was not a novel—at least, it didn't look like one. It appeared to be a sort of ledger.

He reached for it, and a thick cloud of dust rose up as he swiped at the cover. He coughed and sputtered as he lifted it to his eyes.

Two words were embossed on the cover in faded gilt script. Even in the dim light, Arlo could read them clearly: *Town Registry*. He ran a finger along the edge, but before he could open it, he felt an icy hand on his shoulder.

rlo startled and dropped the book. It landed with a thud on top of the desk, sending plumes of dust into the air. He spun round.

Alice stood inches from him, her dark eyes lit with anger. "You shouldn't be here," she said, each word brusque and distinct.

"I—I—" Arlo fumbled for a response that would appear both logical and disarming. "I was hungry and was looking for the kitchen."

Her eyes narrowed. "You are not near the kitchen."

"I realize that, but I don't know where the kitchen is and, no offense, but this house is really confusing. I got lost and ended up here." He lifted his chin defiantly. "I wasn't snooping or anything."

Her eyes flitted to the book on the desk, then to

something behind him, and back to Arlo. She paused a moment, then said, "Come with me."

Arlo followed Alice out of the study, snatching a glance over his shoulder. What had she been looking at? All he could see was a footstool, a statue of a cherub, and a pile of old picture frames leaning against the base of one of the shelves. Before he could make out anything else, Alice closed the door behind them and led Arlo down the hall.

He tried to memorize his way. He thought he just might want to return, but before they had reached the main foyer, he wasn't sure how he'd gotten to the study in the first place, let alone how to find it again.

"Stay here," she said firmly, as though talking to a pet Pomeranian. He nodded as though he were just as compliant.

While he waited, he contemplated the delicate furniture, the faded wallpaper—less faded in some spots than others, he remarked—more oil paintings and old photographs. Something niggled at him. It was close, but kept slipping away.

Alice returned quickly with a pear cored and cut into sections.

"Any chance you have a phone charger?" he asked, wondering if perhaps the Samuelses felt differently about technology.

Alice shook her head, her scraggly hair swaying side to side. "We don't use those here," she said sharply.

She handed Arlo the plate. He took it and thanked her. As he ascended the stairs, he looked over his shoulder. She continued to stare at him until he rounded the corner and was out of sight.

Back in his room, he discovered a fire had been lit. He warmed his hands and feet and then sat down at the table. He ate the fruit, all the while contemplating the conversation he'd overheard, the dusty study, and the wallpaper. Why were some parts of it less faded than others?

He lay on his bed for a moment and closed his eyes. Exhaustion must have overcome him, and he drifted off. He had no idea how long he'd been asleep, but he awoke with a start.

He had been dreaming he was in the woods with his mother and sister. They had been running from something. The ground was uneven, the night dark, and the moon hidden.

As he stumbled along, his foot slipped into a rabbit hole. His ankle turned and snapped—the bone peeking through the flesh just like his mother's had. As he sat cradling his foot, his whole body began to sink into marsh. His mother and Lola were far ahead, dim, fluttering shapes blending into the blackness, as boggy water rose over his head, filling his mouth so he couldn't cry out.

Though Arlo knew it had been a dream, he lay there for some time gasping for air and trying to rid his mind of the horribly real feeling of the dark earth closing in around him. He was just reorienting himself when Lola poked her head into his room to say he should be getting ready for dinner.

"Mrs. Hawthorn says the celebration is going to begin early. Apparently they are *early to bed, early to rise* type folk." She laughed and closed his door.

Unlike Arlo, the rest seemed to have done wonders for his mother. When she limped into his room, he noticed that color had returned to her face. Her cheeks were rosy, and she was grinning ear to ear.

"You seem to be walking better," he said. "How do you feel?"

"Great," said his mother, looking around at his room. "I love this place. I'm sure the B&B I booked isn't half as nice. So, in a way, we're lucky we had that accident."

"*Lucky?*" Arlo scoffed. "How can you say that?"

"Life is never as we expect it to be . . ." Her voice trailed off for a brief moment, but then she continued cheerfully. "If we hadn't had the accident, we certainly would never have come across this lovely place. I'm really happy we did."

"But the car—it's a wreck," he said.

"It was a clunker. We needed a new one, anyway. I'm sure the insurance will give us a few bucks for it. It'll all work itself out. You'll see."

She smiled, and Arlo wondered about the smile. It looked happy and sad and something else entirely all at the same time.

It's going to be okay.

He nodded. They left his room for the celebration.

Any misgivings Arlo had about the people, the town, and the Samuelses' house were temporarily put on hold when he descended the stairs and got a whiff of something tasty. Music echoed through the entire house.

Mrs. Hawthorn greeted them and brought them into a massive room Arlo had missed on his previous wanderings. Hot chestnuts popped and crackled in an iron pan that hung over an open flame in the fireplace. He couldn't recall the last time he'd had freshly roasted chestnuts, but he knew he liked them. The aroma, plus his mother's happiness, lifted his spirits.

At one end of the room was an enormous table set with a white tablecloth, fine china, fancy cutlery, and crystal. Arlo gave a quick calculation and decided the table was set for roughly forty people. At the other end, in an open space, several people milled about.

Lola was already chatting with Hannah and some other kids, while Lovicia sat in a far corner beside Alice. Both were watching him intently.

Arlo saw Simon Sandborn, Doc Brown, and Woodbridge Samuels. He was introduced to Martha and Malachi Lovering and their son, Jacob, and daughter, Isabelle. Martha had a rodent-like face and a high shrill voice Arlo was sure had been one of the voices he'd heard in the hall. Her husband was a fidgety man with ruddy cheeks and buckteeth. There was François Giroux, his wife, Mariette; and her younger brother, Jean; along with Brin Akers, William Weeks, and the twins Nathan and Caleb Russell. In the corner, John Tewksbury entertained with his fiddle, while Levi Dumas played the harmonica.

Arlo was introduced to so many people—thirty, possibly forty—he lost count. Longtime residents going back generations, they said. All seemed nice enough, and yet there was a frostiness to them—a sort of polite unfriendliness. It was as though their warm smiles and formal manners hid their true feelings like sweet perfume masks the stench of sweat.

Of course, the only person who made no effort to hide her disdain was Lovicia. She sat beside Alice, a sour, cantankerous expression emanating from her face. Every time Arlo glanced in her direction, she seemed to be whispering to Alice and shooting daggers at him with her eyes. He was reminded of her words, each syllable sharp and coated with venom.

Leave now. While you still can.

When at last they sat down to dinner, it was nothing like Arlo was expecting. There were platters of corn, bowls of roasted root vegetables and squash puree, but in place of turkey, they were each given a portion of pastry with brown mush.

"What's this?" he said, eyeing the lump on his plate.

"Wild mushroom and herb potpie," said Hannah. "Late summer into early fall is mushroom season in these parts."

"Record rains produced a bumper crop this year," said William Weeks. "We dry them so they gain flavor."

"I especially enjoy the chicken-of-the-woods," said Brin Akers.

"Let me guess," said Arlo's mother. "Tastes like chicken?" Several people chuckled.

"Lovicia foraged for these herself," said Alice. "She's an expert. Knows the edible ones from the poisonous." She glanced at Lovicia.

"P-Poisonous?" said Arlo.

"Oh, Alice is just teasing," said Hannah.

"There are no toxic species in this dish," Doc Brown assured him.

"It's a town specialty," said John Tewksbury. "Goes well with the squash and root vegetables."

Arlo regarded the dish with little enthusiasm.

"Well, it's delicious," said his mother, placing a huge forkful in her mouth, eating heartily. When attention was no longer on her, she turned to Arlo and whispered, "Don't be rude."

Arlo's heart sunk. He knew all about the "turkey pardon"—but pardoning all of them seemed extreme. And the idea of an accidental mushroom poisoning had taken root in his mind, so he sat for long while just staring at the plate.

Lola ate very little. She usually had a robust appetite. All the excitement must have been affecting her stomach.

His mother gave him a nudge. Arlo picked up his fork tentatively. The china dish was so thin, so unlike the clunky dollar-store plates and bowls they had at home, Arlo worried it might shatter if he poked too hard.

Carefully, he scooped up one tiny morsel and placed it just inside his lips, expecting the worst. It was surprisingly tasty. He ate several large mouthfuls, cleaned his plate, and even asked for seconds.

"I can't remember the last time I ate," Arlo heard Martha Lovering chirp from across the table. "This particular dish," she added quickly.

After a dessert of apple crumble, roasted chestnuts, and maple syrup candy, the conversation dwindled and the music lapsed. Several of the guests said their good-byes and began to leave.

"I'm stuffed," said Arlo's mother. "I could use a walk and some fresh air."

"I'd recommend against going out at night," said Woodbridge abruptly. "The trails are complex, and the weather can be highly unpredictable and dangerous this time of year. There are wild animals in these parts who won't think twice about making you their harvest dinner."

Arlo detected a certain amusement in his tone, as though he took pleasure in the warning.

"If it's a walk you wish," he continued, "the corridors are long. I can take you on a tour of the house if you'd like."

Arlo did not like the way his mother smiled at Woodbridge. He was suddenly acutely aware there was no Mrs. Samuels—at least none they had been intro-duced to. He watched his mother take Woodbridge by the arm. Her short, patchy hair was matted on one side, her body thin and brittle, and the cast forced her to limp. Yet she looked happy and at peace for the first time in a long while.

He suddenly felt a sharp pang of guilt for not trusting the town and its inhabitants. He had to admit, it was nice here. The people—other than Lovicia—were friendly. There was nothing sinister about Livermore. It was just different. Remote. He might as well enjoy it, like his mother and Lola, since he'd be leaving the next day.

"Maybe we should go outside," Arlo called to her, as she and Lola headed toward the hallway with Woodbridge.

"It's dangerous," echoed Alice. Then, leaning in close, she whispered, "There are *things* out there. Things you don't want to meet."

Spiders walked across Arlo's shoulders as he turned to face her. "Things? What *things*?"

"Hunters, of course. It's hunting season. Black bear, deer, rabbit . . . Hunters might mistake you for *small* game." A sliver of a grin tugged at her lips.

He stared at her dark eyes a moment. He decided he liked Alice less than Lovicia. He frowned and then hurried to catch up to his mother and Lola.

As Woodbridge showed them around the labyrinth of corridors and rooms, Arlo was led left, then right, up a few steps, then down again, until he was thoroughly con-fused. He'd lost all sense of how the intricate interior of the house matched its relatively simple exterior. Though he was hoping to catch a glimpse of the study, they didn't pass it.

At last, Mr. Samuels returned them to the foyer, and they headed upstairs, Arlo to his room, his mother and Lola to theirs.

The fire had died down, leaving only a red glow sim-mering behind the grate. Arlo lifted an iron poker and prodded the logs, sending a few embers flying. He stood and then drew open the heavy drapes.

A large moon hung suspended in the sky. Stars winked and glittered. His room faced the side of the house. In the pale silver light, he could see the river on one side, the main street on the other. In the distance, mountains rose and fell like silhouettes of sleeping giants.

Arlo removed his phone from his pocket and placed it on the nightstand. He shed his clothes, keeping on only his T-shirt and boxers, and crawled beneath the thick feather down duvet. After several attempts, he found a comfortable position. Exhaustion overcame him, but as he drifted off, Alice's warning reverberated in his brain.

Sometime in the middle of the night, Arlo awoke with the room in darkness. He lay on his side, slightly angled toward the window, one arm bent and tucked beneath his pillow, the other stretched out on the duvet. His eyes were open, but his mind was hazy, walking a tightrope between dream and reality.

It had been a full twenty-four hours since the accident. His limbs still ached, and his bruises were tender. He was thirsty, but it would be too much effort to go to the bathroom to get a drink of water. He was beyond exhausted. He didn't want to move. The bed was so warm, and the air so cold.

A heavy silence pressed in on him. What he wouldn't give for the white noise of traffic, the blare of a siren, or the roar of a jet engine thousands of miles above—anything that signified civilization.

He felt impossibly tired, and yet he lay quiet, staring at the window. Clouds must have blotted out the moon. The glass was dark, like a black mirror, until a pale glimmer shone beyond it. The cloud must be sailing by, Arlo thought.

But then something changed. It started in the bottom right corner of the glass. Dew on the pane was transforming into thin spidery webs of ice spreading steadily upward and outward.

Arlo sat up. The room was cold. Too cold. And not an ordinary middle-of-November kind. This was an odd chill. One that settled deep in his bones and numbed his very heart. He threw off the duvet, rose, and crept to the sill.

He watched wide-eyed as tiny shards of ice continued to spread quickly, covering the entire glass. Its detail was fine and delicate. He reached out to touch it, but just then, he sensed movement on the other side.

Arlo stood frozen, wondering what could possibly be out there. A bird? A rat? He listened, hoping for a familiar squawk or squeal, but could hear only the blood pounding in his ears. He drew in his breath, lifted a trembling hand, and gently rubbed the frigid glass, clearing away a tiny circle. With his heart hammering a warning, he peered out.

For a moment, there was nothing but the cloaked darkness of night. But before he could breathe a sigh of relief, the air was driven from his lungs as a dark shadow moved into the space. For a fleeting moment, something was staring back at him. A grotesquely misshapen face with great glowing eyes.

Jolts of fear electrified his body. Arlo sprang back, pressed himself against the wall, his heart clawing at his chest, his eyes searching wildly side to side. His fists squeezed tight, skin stretched, every sinew and muscle tense with terror.

Seconds passed like hours. His heart beat a million bongs on an invisible clock, until around him the room began to change again. Something in the air was different. Still cold, but it was no longer bone-chilling, heart-numbing.

At last, summoning all his courage, Arlo turned his head and peered back toward the window. The web of frost was melting back to dew, and moonlight shone through the glass, casting a pale beam across the floor.

Arlo forced himself to look out. There was nothing there.

He scrambled back to bed and buried himself beneath the warm duvet. Breathing deeply to calm his nerves, he shut his eyes to the darkness, driving the horrible image so far from his mind it shattered into a million pieces that eventually faded into the nothingness of sleep.

9

Arlo awoke stiff, with that strange sensation of having slept only a short time. He rolled over slowly, yawned, and stretched.

Light was a funny thing. Arlo knew the science of it. He'd studied it in the fourth grade with Mr. Feasby. He was so interested he'd researched it further.

Visible light was only a small part of the electromagnetic spectrum. It was a type of radiant energy that traveled through space in waves, bouncing off objects, allowing humans to see them. Sunlight was very different from moonlight.

Sunlight came directly to objects, whereas moonlight was the sun's reflection. Though the light came from the same source, sunlit objects appeared yellower, whereas the same objects illuminated by the moon appeared bluer. There was another difference, one Arlo could not so easily explain because it involved a feeling, an impression, a mood rather than a physiological phenomenon.

So his room, now filled with golden rays, seemed not only to be yellower, but warmer, happier, more cheerful, less likely to have been the location of such a frightful event as what occurred the previous night, leading Arlo to conclude with near certainty that he had imagined both the frost and the shadowy face.

There was another reason he felt more at ease. It was Friday. His father would be coming that afternoon or early evening. Arlo would not have to spend another night in Livermore. Their ordeal would soon be over.

He lay still for a long time, letting the final chilling fragments of nightmare fly away like so many flakes of sunburnt skin, until the door flung open and Lola skipped inside. She hopped onto his bed, practically bouncing Arlo out of it.

"Look what Hannah made me!"

He examined the cluster of twigs in her hand. "What is *that*?"

"A doll. Isn't she cute?"

The body of the faceless doll was a dried plant stalk. The hair, on what passed for a head, was a clump of roots. The limbs were created with a V-shaped branch attached to the stalk with twine. A tattered piece of cloth wrapped around the body, which Arlo supposed was some sort of dress. *Cute* was definitely not a word that came to mind.

"It's hideous. And you don't even like dolls," he reminded her, pushing the wretched thing away.

What was going on with his sister? First dresses. Now dolls. The only doll Lola had ever owned had been decapitated when she used it as a baseball bat. This girl looked like Lola, but it was as though she'd undergone a personality transplant.

"This is different." She thrust it back toward him. "Hannah made it for me. It's special. I'm calling it Twiggy."

"When did she even have time to make a doll?" he asked, eyeing the alien-looking object suspiciously.

"This morning." Lola combed through the tangle of roots. Bits of crusted earth fell onto the bed.

"What do you mean, *this morning*?" said Arlo, confused, brushing the dirt off the duvet. "It's morning now."

"It's already afternoon. You've been asleep for ages. Mom said you hadn't napped like we did and were exhausted and I wasn't supposed to wake you. She called you Rip Van Winkle."

"Afternoon?" Arlo's heart gave a tremor. He sprang from the bed, grabbing his phone instinctively. Remembering the low battery, he cursed, resisting the urge to turn it on. He pulled on his jeans and sweatshirt, now more pungent than even he was accustomed to.

Lola rolled off the bed. "We're going for a walk. Want to come?"

"You can't go anywhere," he snapped. "Dad's coming. Remember? We should be outside. Waiting. He might already be here looking for us."

"He's not," she said matter-of-factly.

"How do you know?"

"I checked. A bunch of times."

Arlo reached for his jacket and pulled it on.

"It's not like he won't find us here," said Lola. "Not too many places we could be."

Arlo ignored her. He flew from his room, across the hall, and down the steps. He marched past Mrs. Hawthorn and Mr. Samuels without saying a word. He exited the front door and stood in the street searching up and down.

The sky was blue. The sun was shining. There was no one in sight. A bitter wind shepherded a crowd of crusty leaves past him.

He waited a moment longer and then returned to the

porch steps, plunking himself down. After some time, his mother appeared holding a large biscuit and a cup of steaming tea. She handed him the biscuit, then maneuvered herself down to sit beside him.

Her cast appeared to be in good condition, though beneath it, for all he knew, the wound might be festering. How hygienic were Doc Brown's needle and thread? If she didn't get to a proper hospital soon, infection could poison her blood.

"Whatcha doing?" she asked.

"Waiting." He broke a piece off the hard biscuit and popped it into his mouth. It was dry and crumbly.

His mother took a sip of an aromatic herbal tea. "I sure could use a cup of coffee."

A false and fragile normalcy had taken over their lives, as though sitting there, on the porch of the mansion in the isolated town had somehow become ordinary and acceptable.

"There's something about this place," said Arlo, fighting the feeling. "These people . . ."

His mother began to protest, but he cut her off. "I don't mean the lack of technology or other modern stuff. It's something else. I just want Dad to get here."

"Okay," said his mother. "But sitting here in the cold

isn't going to make him get here any quicker. He's notoriously late."

"He's super busy," said Arlo, annoyed. "He'll be here. He promised." He ate another bite of the crumbling biscuit and then kicked at a pebble, sending it flying into the middle of the road.

"You're as stubborn as he is." She grasped the porch railing and hoisted herself up. "If you get too cold, come back inside."

He ate the final bite, wrapped his arms around his chest, and nodded. "It's not so cold. In the sun."

Arlo's mother smiled. She opened the door, out of which strolled Lola and Hannah, holding their stick dolls and giggling. She rolled her eyes, shook her head, and disappeared inside.

"We're going to the mill," said Lola, practically hopping with delight.

Before he could respond, Alice joined them.

"We're going to the mill," echoed Hannah. "Want to come?"

"The mill is old," said Alice. She paused a moment, then added, "And dangerous."

"Yes, yes," said Hannah, waving her hand, "everything around here is old and boring, but I want to show

Lola the barn owls. One had a late clutch. There are still some owlets."

Alice looked at Arlo as though there was something she wanted to add. He hoped it wasn't another creepy warning about *things* lurking in the night or hunters mistaking him for game. He was sure she was the cause of his nightmare.

His nightmare! The face in the glass. How had he been so foolish? Large glowing eyes. Asymmetrical skull. Not a nose, but a beak . . .

He could see it now clearly in his mind's eye. The ghastly, misshapen face in the window resolved itself into what it really was—a big old barn owl. The woods must be full of them. He suddenly felt ridiculous for having been so frightened. Maybe Lola was right. Maybe he was scared of everything.

"You shouldn't take her inside the mill," said Alice. "It isn't safe. It's dilapidated. You wouldn't want her to get hurt, would you?" There was a haunted look in her eyes, as though she was expecting doom to arrive at any moment.

"You're such a worrywart." Hannah laughed. She tossed her a look of childish contempt. Whereas Alice appeared haunted, Hannah looked hungry. She took

Lola's hand. "Come on." They began strolling up the street, giggling and acting silly with their matching stick dolls.

"We should go with them," said Alice. "The timbers are rickety."

Arlo eyed her, then the road. The girls were racing each other. They were already on the railroad tracks heading toward the mill.

It was vital that he remain visible in the street, waiting for his father's arrival, but he needed to protect his sister as well. Perhaps he could do both. He could keep one eye on Lola and the other out for his father.

His mother was probably right. Chances were, his father would be a little later than promised. Arlo stood and dusted the crumbs from his jeans. Then he and Alice hurried toward the railway tracks.

As he walked, he couldn't escape the strange sensation he was wandering in a dream. Not one of those cheerful dreams where you felt light and carefree, where you could run fast, jump high—even fly. And not a nightmare either. There were no monsters or surprise math tests lurking around a corner. No dark shadows or animals giving chase.

No. It was more like one of those dreams where

everything was normal, where you could swear the dream was real except for tiny things, just distorted enough, just tilted enough, just blurry enough to feel wrong.

"No offense," said Arlo, "but your town's really small."

Alice glanced sideways at him. He couldn't quite read her expression. "Yes. It is."

"So," he added casually, "what do you do for excitement around here?"

Alice's gaze panned the surroundings. "Excitement?" She sighed. "Seems like centuries since we had any excitement around here."

There was a hint of bitterness to her voice, so he let the topic drop. He tried a few more questions, but she provided only clipped responses in a voice devoid of emotion, so Arlo gave up. Clearly, small talk was not Alice's strength.

The sun had passed its zenith. It was viciously bright. Arlo guessed by its position that it was midafternoon. The further east you were, the earlier the sun set. There would only be another two, maximum three hours before dark.

The cloudless sky shimmered blue, highlighting the bleakness of the dilapidated wooden structures and the abandoned rusted railway tracks. They wandered past the old depot—the lettering still visible: SAWYER RIVER STATION. There were a general store and a post office that Alice explained were closed for the holiday weekend.

Following the extensive network of tracks, they made their way down to the mill. Enormous stacks of dark, rotting lumber lay piled as high as houses. An old boxcar was half covered in tall grass and creeping shrubs. The remains of an old trestle crossed the river in the distance. Arlo could hear the gurgling rush of water.

The mill itself was a massive structure still more or less intact. There was a loading platform attached to what appeared to be three or four connected buildings of various sizes with slanting and sagging roofs. Tracks wound around the mill on either side, and behind it, Arlo caught a glimpse of the pond. A mountain of old logs descended the hill. In the distance they were like match-sticks dropped into a jumbled heap. It was as though the great mill had simply shut down at midday and folks had just walked away, leaving everything untouched behind.

Hannah and Lola had already begun climbing the wooden steps to the loading platform.

"Lola," called Arlo, "we shouldn't go inside." But it was too late. She was already gone.

He climbed the rickety steps and stood on the

platform. He had to step gingerly around gaping holes where planks had rotted through.

Inside the building, he was met with a sigh of dank, musty air. The taste of ash and decay was bitter in his mouth. Pale light leaked through gaps in the warped siding. The floorboards were gray and moldy and covered in sawdust, the ceiling and corners dripping with spiderwebs. Spindly-legged bodies scurried into shadows. There were piles of rotting boards and logs everywhere.

"This isn't the original mill," said Alice, her voice muffled and hollow. "The first burnt to the ground. The second burnt as well. This is the third, and it hasn't been used in a long time."

Arlo tried to imagine what the mill might have looked like bustling with workmen and freshly felled trees. With hollering and laughter. With life. But he couldn't see it. What he saw was death and decay—like the heaps of black logs that would never become fine furniture, flooring, or house frames.

On the ground near her feet, a large moth struggled, flapping its wings but unable to fly. He watched as Alice lifted her foot and flattened the creature.

"Why did you do that?" he asked, startled by the harshness of her action.

Her eyes rose rapidly to meet his. "It was the right

thing to do," she said, too quickly for his liking. "It would have died a slow death. A quick one was merciful."

Before he had time to consider her words or respond, Lola was shouting.

"Look! Look!" Lola pointed to the rafters. There was a gray clump. Feathered heads poked out. "The nest!"

"Barn owls don't have nests," said Hannah. "Not made of sticks and branches, anyway. They find planks or hollows and use their pellets."

"Pellets?" asked Lola.

"Anything they can't digest—like bones, fur, beaks, teeth—turn into pellets they regurgitate," said Alice.

"Lovely," said Arlo.

"They break up the pellets and make a sort of nest," added Hannah.

"So basically, they live in their own vomit," said Arlo.

"That's disgusting," said Lola.

Just then, they heard a long, harsh scream. It echoed all around them. There was movement, so sudden and swift, they hardly had time to react. Sharp talons and giant wings swooped toward them.

"Duck!" shouted Arlo.

At once, all four dove through a doorway, collapsing into separate heaps on the other side. Here, there were more stacks of logs and planks and what appeared to be a large frame with a giant blade. Arlo thought it reminded him of a guillotine except the blade was vertical and serrated.

A thick plank was being sliced by the giant saw, which seemed to have come to a stop midway. There were so many cogs and levers. Arlo could see through a rotted plank below to the river, where there was a great wheel that he assumed powered the saw.

Lola was rolling on the ground roaring with laughter. "You said duck—but it's an owl!"

"Watch out!" shouted Arlo, as she rolled toward a brittle, broken board.

Lola stopped short of the gap, but the doll slipped from her hand and fell through the hole. "Twiggy!" she shouted, putting her face into the gap. "I have to get her." She scrambled to her feet and, with Hannah by her side, retraced her steps outside.

Arlo was fascinated with the saw. He put his hand on the thick serrated blade. Then he ran it along the plank, feeling where the saw had made its cut.

"Don't touch that," said Alice.

Arlo could hear Hannah's and Lola's voices echoing up through the floorboards. They were below them now, near the river and the enormous wheel. He bent to call to her, but something held his arm. For a moment, he thought it was Alice, but she was standing in front of him. He turned to see the sleeve of his jacket was caught on a splinter between the blade and the plank.

The girls' voices drifted up. "I've got her!" Lola was yelling happily.

"The wheel!" shouted Hannah. "The wheel!"

Then three things happened all at once.

There was a sound—like a pipe being struck by metal—followed by an awful groaning and scraping of rusted parts that hadn't moved in ages. And for a moment, Arlo felt as if the entire mill might collapse. The wheel beneath them was moving. He turned in horror to see the blade slowly begin to descend. He yanked, but his jacket wedged tighter, being drawn toward the saw.

Shock drove the air from his lungs. He yanked hard, but his sleeve wouldn't budge. The blade was picking up speed, moving downward, drawing him inward. Fear froze his muscles. He stood wide-eyed, unable to think or scream, watching as the blade moved closer and closer to his hand.

And then he felt it. Pulling and pushing. It was Alice. She was shoving him closer to the blade! His body reacted instinctively, wrestling her with his free hand, but she was strong. She was going to win.

"Stop . . . struggling . . ." Alice commanded, but he continued to battle.

The zipper on his jacket was lowered, and in a second, he was free and away from the blade that ripped through the cuff of his sleeve as though it were paper.

The grinding stopped. The blade halted. Alice's lips were moving, but it was taking his brain some time to catch up.

"I told you not to touch that," she snapped.

He glared at her. "What were you trying to do to me?"

"What do you think?" she said flatly.

Arlo replayed the scene in his mind. Had she tried to help him? Or hurt him? He couldn't quite settle on a definitive response, so he pushed past her, reached out a trembling hand, and, yanking with all his might, pulled his jacket free. The cuff was destroyed, but his hand was intact.

Alice turned abruptly, and he followed her out of the sawmill. Lola and Hannah were waiting for them.

"You nearly got my hand sliced off," he said, still fuming.

"What?" Lola gasped. "How?"

"The saw was moving," he said. "My sleeve got caught."

Alice regarded Hannah steadily, her expression stony.

"I'm sorry. It was an accident," said Hannah, her cheeks flushing. "I leaned against the wheel. The wood block in the cog must have come loose."

"I stopped it," said Lola proudly. "I wedged it with a piece of plank."

"Are you okay?" he said, taking his sister by the hand and drawing her toward him. Her hair was a mess, her knee bruised, and he noticed a circular cut on the side of her neck. It couldn't be fresh, as it was already scabbed over. A remnant of the accident.

"I saved Twiggy." She held up the stick doll and flashed a large toothy grin.

Arlo frowned. "Come on. Let's get out of here."

With his nerves still humming, he dragged Lola back to the Samuels Mansion, and when the three girls went inside, he sat back down on the porch steps and waited patiently. But as the sun melted into the horizon, anger began to rise like bile in his throat. Where was his father? He had promised he'd be here.

Arlo withdrew his phone from his pocket. If he could manage to get another signal, he could call. He had been near the Samuels Mansion when he found the signal last time. He could try again. Powering up the phone sucked up battery power. He was at five percent.

Eyeing the device, he began to walk. He moved this way and that, hoping for a signal. The battery dropped to four percent. He moved quicker. Down the hill toward Lovicia's, then back up. Three percent. Two. A bar flickered briefly. His hopes rose and then fell. The battery was dead. The phone powered down.

Arlo kicked himself. How stupid he'd been to waste the battery like that. He plunked himself down and watched as the sun dipped lower and lower into the horizon.

Arlo's mother tried several times to coax him inside. He refused. She even brought him his dinner outside. A bowl of corn chowder made with Thanksgiving leftovers. How he wished it were a turkey club sandwich with a side of stuffing.

A twilit glow swept the landscape. Soon all light would be gone. He took a deep breath. If he couldn't hold it together now, how would he fare once all light drained?

His anger grew stronger and hotter. He had always defended his father. Always. How could he abandon them here?

Arlo's thoughts skipped liked stones. Fragments of memories played out before his mind's eye like a film reel in fast-forward motion, flitting from scene to scene, each one awakening more and more anger.

There was the time his father had missed Take Your Father to School Day. While all the other fathers spoke at the front of the class about their jobs, Arlo watched the door nervously. The minutes ticked by, but his father never came. There were countless missed sporting events—including a Little League championship—and for his ninth birthday, he received a check for one hundred dollars in a card. The usual *presents* instead of *presence*. Once his father messed up the schedule and completely forgot to pick him and Lola up from school. They'd waited over an hour in the pouring rain before his mother finally arrived.

Even when he was physically there, he wasn't there emotionally. Arlo tried so many times to tell him how he felt—about how scared he was—but each time, it resulted in a lot of advice and lectures. Arlo never felt like his father truly listened or understood or validated his feelings.

He'd always made excuses for his father. Always taken his word. His side. If only Arlo hadn't drained the battery, he could call his father right now and blast him for being late. For being thoughtless and insensitive. If only they had an outlet and a charger in this backward broken-down town.

An idea settled into Arlo's stomach like an accidentally

swallowed peach pit. As it developed, it churned up bitterness, making him slightly queasy. If he could get back to the car, perhaps he could start it. It was in no condition to drive, but perhaps it could still do something. Perhaps it could charge his phone.

It was a good plan, but it would mean heading out into the dark woods. At night. Alone. The more he thought about it, the more anxious he became.

In the distance, the trees loomed large and a lone crow circled, squawking. What was that old saying? One for sorrow . . .

It was late by the time Arlo gave up on his father and accepted he wasn't coming. His mother had said they had no choice but to spend another night at the Samuels Mansion, and though Arlo agreed, he didn't tell her he would not be sleeping.

10

A rlo flung back his duvet. He had lain there, fully clothed, waiting nervously for the moment everyone would be asleep. Finally, he could wait no longer.

He crept to the door, silent as a thief, and slipped out into the hall. The house was so quiet it was as though it were holding its breath. Carefully, he tiptoed down the steps, and before anyone in the Samuelses' house was the wiser, he was out the front door and on his way.

Livermore was a dismal enough place in the daytime, but at night, it was as bleak and desolate and unwelcoming as a tomb. The sky was clear. A gibbous moon hung like a silver pendant against the velvety black dress of night. It bathed the homes in a pallid glow.

The air was piercingly cold but calm. Steamy puffs

escaped Arlo's mouth and nostrils as he hurried down the street, past Simon Sandborn's, Lovicia's, and the rest of the rickety structures. In the moonlight, he worried he might be seen, but all the homes were dark and still.

As Arlo stepped inside the covered bridge, the timbers whined and complained. Despite the cold, the scent of rot was heavy. He could taste it on his lips as he trod lightly but quickly, exiting on the other side of the river.

Reaching the top of the embankment, Arlo hopped over the low wall and paused a moment. He figured he had roughly three, possibly four miles to the car and then the return journey. He could do it in a couple hours if he hurried.

He glanced at the town. There was still time to turn back. But if he didn't charge his phone and reach help, they'd be stuck in Livermore and his mother would not get the care she required. He'd once read about an infected break that turned septic. Bacteria entered the bloodstream and shut down the organs. It could happen quickly and with little warning. He forced the thought from his mind and disappeared beneath the canopy of intertwining limbs.

The woods were darker and tighter than he remembered. He picked up his pace, following the path as it twisted and turned. Thick trunks of ancient trees stood like sentinels crowding either side. The cold bit into his exposed flesh as he jogged at a steady pace. He was lucky it wasn't windy, or he'd have risked frostbite.

Around him, the shadows were cavernous. Once or twice, out of the corner of his eye, he thought he caught sight of something shifting, but when his head snapped in that direction, all was still.

"Owls," he told himself, forcing other—more frightening—thoughts from his mind.

When the path ahead widened, Arlo knew he would reach the fork soon. Despite the heat his body was generating from the movement, he felt increasingly cold. There was a dampness to the air. Though the sky was clear, he knew snow was on its way. Once he reached the car, he could get another sweatshirt, as well as his gloves and knit cap. The thought of warm, fresh clothes propelled him onward.

At last, Arlo arrived at the old sign that pointed to Livermore. He paused, swallowing great gulps of air until his breathing slowed. He had never been a good runner, and he had reached his limit. He'd have to walk the rest of the way.

The road was as desolate as it had been two nights before. Not a single car passed in either direction. He walked with steady, purposeful strides until from a distance he could see their car. Crumpled and broken against the enormous tree, the vehicle sat like a strange portrait, a tableau of that awful moment. And yet it was somehow a comforting sight. He raced the remaining steps.

The trunk of the car was ajar. Arlo's suitcase was unzipped, his clothes strewn about. He stepped out of his shoes, located an extra pair of thick wool socks, and pulled them over the ones he was wearing. His shoes felt a little snug, but it was worth it. Next, he found his favorite fleece sweatshirt, removed his jacket, and pulled the fleece over the sweatshirt he was wearing. He found his knit cap, yanked it over his ears, and with his jacket back on, he already felt warmer.

He walked round the side of the car and stared at the driver's seat. His mother's smashed phone lay beneath it on the floor mat covered in brown dried blood. He choked back a sob. This was no time for emotions. Climbing in, Arlo positioned himself behind the wheel.

The old Buick did not have a USB port like modern vehicles, but it did have a cigarette lighter that, with the help of an adapter, did the trick. The cable still hung limp from it, waiting to provide service. He dug his phone out of his pocket and connected it.

Arlo had little interest in cars, and though he had

studied the online manual for safety purposes, he had never paid much attention to the mechanics of driving. He knew his friend's cars all started with a fob and the push of a button, but the old Buick still used a key. It was in the ignition.

Arlo's fingers trembled with anticipation as he gave it a twist. The engine groaned, struggling to turn over. He pumped the gas like he'd seen his mother do and tried again. The engine coughed once, twice, but then died.

Arlo tried several more times, all to no avail. Tears prickled his eyes. He blinked them away. The car had been his only hope. He punched the steering wheel in frustration, which only served to hurt his hands.

Then, glancing around, he saw Lola's tablet and a half-eaten brown apple on the floor of the back seat. She'd been eating the apple and playing a game when the accident happened. He reached down and picked it up.

The screen was cracked, but it powered on without problem. Unfortunately, she had no data, and there was no Wi-Fi to tap into for a text. It still had fifty percent battery life. If only he could syphon the power from it to his phone.

"That's it!" he shouted, tossing the tablet aside.

He exited the car and dashed back to the trunk. He found his sister's suitcase, unzipped it, and began rifling frantically through her things until he found what he was looking for. Lola had a bright pink Betty Boop wash purse she'd gotten for her birthday last year. It came with a toothbrush, a bar of soap, some hand sanitizer, and of all things . . . an external charger.

The charger was attached to the inside of the purse with thin black ribbon. Arlo ripped it out easily and held it in the palm of his hand. The credit-card-sized object was covered in silky material with hearts and stars and sayings like *Let's go!* and *You energize me!* and *Charge it!*

One end sported two short white wires: a USB and a lightning cable. He went back to the car, retrieved his phone, and connected it to the charger. Because the phone was completely dead, he knew it would take some time, so he plunked himself on the cooler on the side of the road and waited.

Despite adrenaline and his new clothing, Arlo was cold again. Time passed. The screen remained black. The chill increased.

When he'd given it enough time, he sucked in his breath and held it. As he gently pressed the Home button, his eyes were greeted with the familiar lightning bolt. For a moment he just stared at the screen. Then a surge of joy ignited his body. He sprang to his feet and punched the air in jubilation. He had done it. He had cleared the first hurdle. The phone was charging.

It would take some time before the phone would actually turn on. He had no idea how much power was in the charger, and he wasn't about to waste a nanosecond of battery life by continuously trying the phone, so he made sure the attachment was secure, placed both objects in his pocket, and began the journey back to Livermore.

The dull *clip clip* of Arlo's footsteps on the dirt road seemed to echo around him, giving him the impression someone else was walking nearby. More than once, he stopped, searched behind, and listened. The limbs of the trees creaked and moaned, though there wasn't any wind. The old forest, deep in slumber, had come awake.

Then, in the distance, a loud cry—something halfway between wail and groan—split the silence. Arlo stiffened. It was like no other sound he'd heard before. Not an owl. Or a wolf. It came from nothing he recognized. The air echoed for several seconds.

The surge of happiness he'd felt only moments ago drained like water from a sieve. It was replaced with cold, wet dread that pooled in the pit of his stomach. He had to get out of the dark woods. He had to get back to his mother and sister.

In his excitement, Arlo had forgotten all about his gloves. The air bit at his exposed cheeks and hands. His muscles, already aching from the journey there, protested each step. Still, he forged ahead.

At the fork, Arlo turned brusquely and headed down the road that led to Livermore. All the while, he sharpened his senses to every sound, every movement, every touch to his skin, real or imagined.

Once again, the road dwindled until it was little more than a path. Giant trees closed in around him, hugging the edges, looming overhead, their twisted boughs reaching downward like brittle fingers. He picked up his pace.

Halfway to the covered bridge, the snap of a twig drew his attention. He froze. In his peripheral vision, he caught movement. Something was there—a stain in the darkness, something large and unrecognizable.

Arlo's first instinct was to run. Instead, as if willed by the force of a faint memory, he turned slowly to face the shadow. His jaw slackened as his brain grasped the shape and molded sense of it.

There, no more than ten feet in front of him, stood a moose. But not just any moose. This was the moose they had hit.

Both he and the beast remained statue still, assessing each other. There was no doubt in Arlo's mind—this was the one. It was missing a paddle, and its thick dark fur was matted near the hind leg. But there was something else. Something strange. Arlo was drawn to it, like a fly to rotting flesh.

Slowly, steadily, he approached the creature. It was massive—as tall as an NBA basketball player and weighing at least a ton. But there was something even more astonishing.

Moonlight streaked through the branches, casting stripes of light across the animal's dark fur. Where the light touched, a ghostly glow seemed to emanate from beneath the thick coat. Arlo drew nearer.

Up close, he felt as small and as insignificant as a flea. If this creature decided to charge him, he'd be no match. He gathered his courage, reached out a tremulous hand, and touched the hide. It was blisteringly cold, practically burning his fingertips. He snatched them back instinctively.

Just then, the moose startled. It regarded Arlo with milky white eyes. He braced himself, but the animal merely twitched and then bounded off, disappearing into the brush.

Arlo rubbed his fingertips. Feeling was returning to them. He wondered what had startled the animal. He was about to continue on his path when the hair suddenly rose on his arms. He had the distinct feeling he wasn't alone.

Another earsplitting cry cut through the silence— closer, more urgent—and a stench filled the air—animal-like. His first thought came rapidly and in a single frightening word: *bear!*

Forgetting all he knew about staying safe during bear encounters, Arlo bolted as fast as his legs could carry him. Dried leaves crunched beneath his feet as he scrambled off the path and straight into the woods.

He darted this way and that, further and further into the darkness, dodging trunks and ducking limbs, heading deeper and deeper, not stopping for a moment to see if the creature—if it even was a bear—was following. Yet, the faster he ran, the more the forest seemed to stand still—as though it were folding in around him.

Arlo's chest began to ache. His joints dulled and slowed like rusty machinery, until at last, he could run no longer. He dipped behind a large trunk covered in a thick skin of oily black lichen and pressed his back to it, hoping he was safely hidden.

He'd meant to catch his breath, but instead, the last bit of oxygen was driven from his lungs by the ghastly sight that lay ahead.

PART TWO

ALICE

11

lice lay awake in her bed. A gathering had been
called. It would happen at midnight. Everyone
was expected to attend. Even the folks from Little
Canada. A decision must be made.

She yawned deeply. She was tired. Tired of town
meetings. Tired of the same people, the same food, and
the same discussions. Just plain tired.

A bitter wind pressed against her window. The old
wooden frame creaked and groaned. It was getting
colder. Soon it would snow. Perhaps even the next day.
She longed to feel the crisp cold of a deep winter's night.
To feel the stifling heat of a sticky sweet summer day. To
feel anything at all.

The arrival of these people had awakened something
inside her—something that had been lost. How upset

Arlo was over his mother's injury. How excited Lola was over every trivial thing Hannah showed her. Alice had felt neither disappointment nor delight, neither sorrow nor rage in such a long while she was surprised, and not altogether upset, to sense a slight prickle of envy.

Alice's thoughts etched circular patterns in her head. They went round and round, spiraling back to the night that now felt like ten lifetimes ago. The night everything had changed. Even then, envy had been her downfall.

That night, Alice could not sleep either. She had lain in bed stewing over her birthday. The next day she would turn twelve, and she was madder than a hornet.

Her sister, Libby, had had the loveliest of birthdays when she had turned twelve less than two years before. Mama had taken her all the way to Boston and bought Libby a costly and beautiful cream satin dress with a ruby-red sash and shiny black patent-leather shoes.

There had been a grand party—the whole town had been invited. They'd had raspberry cake, strawberry rhubarb pie, and ice-cold lemonade. The children had played games like Graces, Drop the Handkerchief, and croquet while the adults enjoyed friendly chatter. Libby had looked stunning—the center of attention—with her hair in perfect ringlets and her beautiful satin dress.

Alice pressed her thin lips together. It wasn't fair.

There would be no trip to Boston for her. No grand party. No perfect ringlets. And no special dress.

Papa had gone to Lincoln the day before to deal with a group of choppers that had been wrongfully jailed. Old Mr. Henry had sent the sheriff to arrest them on account of he said they had crossed the divide between the two company holdings. Alice overheard Papa say that Old Henry was even forcing his men to live within the boundaries of Livermore in order to form a majority to vote in favor of redefining property lines.

With Papa gone, Mama had been all flustered. She had been occupying herself with the care of Libby, who had taken ill shortly after a trip to the city. Libby was fatigued and experiencing aches and pains. Alice couldn't help but feel her sister had somehow contrived this mysterious malady to steal her thunder.

Alice would have told her sister so, except Libby had been confined to her room for several days now. Only Mama was allowed into the room to tend to her. Even Papa hadn't been permitted to see her. Mrs. Hawthorn placed trays of food outside the door, having been instructed to have no contact with her either.

Alice had stood in the hallway earlier that day, watching Mama open the door just wide enough to pull the tray inside. Later, she had placed it in the hall again, the food barely touched. Alice could hear Mrs. Hawthorn and her mother talking in hushed whispers from either side of the door. Then Mrs. Hawthorn reclaimed the tray using white gloves that she promptly laundered.

How extreme it all seemed. All this fuss for what was most likely a few sniffles. Why, not one month prior, Alice had experienced a horrible case of effluvium, and no one had been in a tizzy over her. She had had severe abdominal pain and been absolutely certain she was dying. When Doc Brown examined her, however, he merely advised her not to eat quite so much of Mrs. Hawthorn's maple baked beans.

"Libby." Alice sighed. It was just like her sister, always the belle of the ball, the apple of everyone's eye.

Doc Brown had come to see Libby the day before Papa left, and shortly after, of all things, a photographer arrived! At first, Alice had believed it was for her—a portrait in honor of her twelfth birthday—but just imagine, even ill, Mama felt it more important to photograph her lovely Libby.

Alice had lain there that night, her emotions simmering and stewing like a pot of Mrs. Hawthorn's scotch broth. No trip. No new dress. Unless . . .

That was when the thought lodged itself in the darkest part of her mind. It was a brilliant idea. Perhaps there wouldn't be a new dress, but there was no reason Alice couldn't wear something special.

Slowly, stealthily, she slipped out of bed. The fire had long died, and only the ashes lay smoldering in the fireplace. The house was cold and dark. Alice's body gave an involuntary shudder.

Carefully, she opened her door. It whined and whimpered, but there was no one to hear its complaints. Stepping as lightly as a ballerina, she tiptoed down the hall toward her sister's room.

Pausing a moment, Alice placed an ear to Libby's door. She could hear her sister's labored breathing. She had always been so fragile. So delicate. It bordered on annoying.

Alice turned the handle at barely noticeable increments and opened the door. The curtains were drawn, and the room was black as pitch. A rank odor, like bile, saturated the air. She held her breath.

Libby's room was quite a bit larger than Alice's. Her bed was off to the side, and an enormous armoire loomed opposite. Alice worried her mother might be in the room, but luckily there was no shadow in the great armchair that had been positioned beside the bed. She must be sleeping in one of the guest rooms.

Gradually, so as not to disturb Libby's slumber, Alice

crept toward the armoire. She'd have to be quick, or she just might wake her. Swinging open the heavy doors, Alice rifled through the clothing hanging inside. It was difficult to find what she was looking for in the darkness, but when her fingers found the silky cloth, she knew at once it was the dress.

Just then, Libby moaned, and Alice stiffened. She held her breath as her sister murmured unintelligibly. Then, at last, she shifted in her bed and was breathing heavily once again.

Alice stood frozen a long moment. When she was certain Libby was fast asleep, she removed the dress from the armoire, and without a backward glance, she fled the room.

Alice lit an oil lamp and held the buttery soft fabric against her so that it covered her bedclothes. She stared at herself in the mirror that hung over her dresser. She wouldn't need her mother, her father, or even Libby to have a special birthday. She'd make it special all on her own.

The next morning was bright and sunny, but there was a chill in the air that whispered of winter. Alice would have to head out while the sun would provide some warmth. She would not waste any time.

She dipped a rough cloth in the washbasin on her dresser and washed her face, scrubbing her cheeks particularly hard to give them a rosy hue. Next, she brushed her teeth with a bone and pig-bristle brush Papa had purchased from a peddler and tooth powder consisting of alum, ground eggshells, brimstone, and baking powder. It had a hint of cinnamon to freshen her breath.

She ran a comb through her long hair. She plaited it into French braids that crowned her face and hung down the sides of her shoulders. She had always had a special knack for weaving her hair.

Finally, she slipped into the silky cream dress and tied the red sash tightly around her waist, doing her best to create a large elaborate bow at the back. She slid her hands down the fabric of the skirt, admiring herself in the mirror.

She looked just as lovely as Libby. Perhaps lovelier. With her head high, Alice traipsed past her sister's room, down the steps, and into the dining room.

"Good morning, Miss Alice," said Mrs. Hawthorn, wiping the table with a damp rag. "How are you today?"

"Very well, thank you," Alice chirped. "What a lovely day this is."

Mrs. Hawthorn made a vinegary face. "I know it's your birthday, Miss Alice, but you ought not to be so cheerful given your sister's worsening condition. Her body is burning up. Your mother's sent for Doc Brown again. He will be by this afternoon . . ."

"I see," said Alice thoughtfully. "Well, it's possible she's merely avoiding the geography assignment Mrs. Abbott expects today. Libby hates geography." She turned to leave, but Mrs. Hawthorn gripped her shoulder.

"She's quite ill," said the woman sharply. "The mouth sores have begun."

Alice wriggled from her grasp. She did not know what mouth sores meant, but it sounded revolting. "I'll be sure to let Mrs. Abbott know."

She flitted out the door like a bird whose cage had been left ajar before Mrs. Hawthorn could halt her or say anything further to ruin her day.

The morning light peeked through the birch and spruce with a false promise of warmth. As she stepped into the misleading sunshine, a crisp wind cut through the fine dress, chilling Alice to the bone. Still, she was determined not to wear a coat, as it might crinkle her dress. She had wanted absolutely everyone she passed to see her and admire how lovely she looked.

"Hello, Mr. Sandborn," she called politely. "Good morning, Mrs. Nesmith." She waved exaggeratedly. "What a fine fall day, Mr. Little . . ." She twirled. "The weather is much better today, don't you think, Mrs. Giroux?"

And so she had skipped along, as though walking across the sky instead of through the village. She swished and sashayed past the general store and the post office, drawing as much consideration as she could from the elderly men and women sitting on the benches gossiping. She then backtracked, meandering toward the school-house, where, outside, a group of children waited impatiently for Mrs. Abbott to ring the bell.

Papa had wanted Alice and Libby to go to private school in town. But Mama had insisted they stay in the village and go to school with the other children. Mama loved the girls more than life itself and couldn't bear the thought of being so far from them. Libby agreed with Mama, as always, but Alice felt as though she were being held prisoner in the dreary place where slow rot threatened to eat away at her from the inside.

"What's she all done up for?" muttered Caleb Russell.

"Who wears a satin dress to school?" scoffed Jonathan Tyler.

"Spoiled rich girl," said Phoebe Fox.

"That's who," said Isabelle Lovering.

The other children adored Libby, but they disliked Alice and did little to conceal this fact. They whispered about her behind her back and weren't shy to say cruel things to her face.

Never let them see you care, Alice told herself, holding her head high as she strolled past the gaggle of gray faces glaring at her with hateful eyes. She squinted, keeping her own eyes open just enough to see where she was going, but in her mind she was elsewhere. She was walking through a green field full of daffodils rimmed with white lilac bushes, their fresh floral scent filling her thoughts,

"Aw, pay them no mind," said Hannah, taking Alice by the hand. "You look Jim-dandy. Happy birthday."

Hannah was different from the others. She was never envious. Never hateful. The closest to kind any of them could be. Alice had the impression Hannah felt as trapped in the drudgery of their colorless existence as she did.

Mrs. Abbott stepped onto the porch and rang the entry bell, and the two girls brushed past and into the building.

"Happy birthday, Alice," said Mrs. Abbott. "You look lovely. How's Libby today?"

"I'm afraid she's still not well," said Alice primly.

"Oh, poor dear," said the teacher. "Do give her my best wishes for a speedy recovery."

Alice nodded and then sighed, and the teacher mistook this as worry for her sister, not frustration for herself. Even now. Even today. Libby was still drawing all the attention.

Alice primped her skirt and then took her place in the fourth row of wooden seats. She barely listened while reciting her lessons. Somehow, the day wasn't going quite as she'd hoped. All day long, she continued to run her hands along the buttery fabric of her sister's dress.

"Now," said the teacher. "Before we head out for the day, I want you all to shake hands with Alice and wish her the happiest of days." She invited Alice to stand at the door.

At last, thought Alice, the focus would be on her. She stood perfectly stiff and straight, beaming as all the children beginning with the younger ones, right up to the twins, Nathan and Jacob Russell, were made to shake her hand and wish her well. Only Hannah's little sister slipped past the long line, sticking out her tongue and laughing as Hannah gave Alice a tight squeeze. It certainly wasn't a grand party, but it was something.

The sun had disappeared behind the clouds and the afternoon was much colder. Alice walked briskly, hugging her arms to her chest. Perhaps, she thought, she might catch a cold and then her mother and Mrs. Hawthorn might fuss over her.

She entered the house, but before she made it to the stairs, she heard Papa call to her. She stopped and swung round, elated. He had made it home for her birthday after all!

"Alice, I must tell you something . . ." he said, a grave expression carved into his features, as though he was about to impart something quite serious. But then, seeing her bright smile, his expression softened. "Why, it's your birthday, my dear. I'm so sorry. I'd nearly forgotten."

His arms enveloped her, holding her close, feeling

the silkiness of her satin sleeves. And then, as if noticing for the first time, he let loose of the cloth as if it might burn him and backed away. He stared at her, horror-stricken.

"Oh, Alice," he gasped. "What have you done?"

A lice could do nothing but wait. And hope. And pray. Libby was much worse, and Mama had already taken ill. She was being tended to by both Mrs. Hawthorn and Papa.

No one, save for Doc Brown, dared enter the home. He had made several trips already, but each time his expression seemed grimmer and his whispers more urgent.

Two weeks had passed since Alice's birthday—the day she had paraded about town in the infected dress, placing all those who came in contact with her in jeopardy. If the others had disliked her before, they despised her now. And though she had apologized until her throat was raw, she could escape neither shame nor blame.

Doc Brown had said it would be a miracle if even half

those she had come into close contact with managed to avoid the illness that British historian Thomas Babington Macaulay called "the most terrible of all the ministers of death . . . turning a babe into a changeling at which the mother shuddered and making the eyes and cheeks of the betrothed maiden objects of horror to the lover."

"The poet Orinda phrases it best," he told Papa. He quoted a stanza:

That fierce Disease, which knows not how to spare
The young, the Great, the Knowing, or the Fair.

Alice lamented her horrible choice. But no matter the tears, no matter the justifications, pretenses, or regrets, she could do nothing to reclaim her reckless actions.

"I'm sorry," she had said to her father a thousand times over. "I'm so very terribly sorry . . ."

The photograph of Libby arrived via post the same day she died. Simon Sandborn had fetched it from the post office and delivered the envelope, placing it on the porch. Mama clutched the photograph and wept bitter tears, which fell on the paper that still showed Libby's face clear and beautiful, free from the fluid-filled lesions that had ravaged her like grains of rice beneath her skin. She wore the dress Alice had stolen to her grave.

Later that day, Alice was stricken with fever. It came on so quick and sudden, she was bedridden by midafternoon. She lay there, drifting between unconsciousness and delirium, and in her mind, she heard her father and Doc Brown talking in hushed whispers outside her door. She thought she could make out what they were saying, though she could not be certain whether it was real or a figment of her tormented mind.

"We shall have to dig wide and deep," said Doc Brown.

"Then it must be done now. Before the snow comes," said her father. "Before the ground is too hard. Before we are all incapable of wielding a shovel. Simon Sandborn has agreed to help. François Giroux as well."

"Forty in total," said Doc Brown. "We must make it large enough to fit us all."

14

Days passed, though Alice couldn't be sure of the exact time. It seemed to meld and merge like a wet watercolor, minutes and hours oozing together until life was nothing but one long stretch of painful existence. With her drapes drawn, she could be certain of neither night nor day.

Dig wide and deep . . . The terrifying words echoed in the far recesses of her consciousness.

In the grips of her confusion and frenzy, an absurd thought wriggled itself free, seeping out of her brain dark and unwanted. She forced it back in, but it tunneled in circles until it was all she could think of. She had to go there. She had to see it for herself.

Her body burned with fever. She twisted and writhed, somehow finding the physical strength and mental fortitude to drag herself from her bed. In nothing but her nightshirt, she staggered along the hall, down the steps, and out the front door.

The wind was icy, but it was such a relief against her fiery skin. She closed her eyes and let it envelop her, wrap her in its icy tendrils.

She resisted the urge to let go, to fall to the ground and allow the cold take her. She had to get there. She had to see it with her own eyes.

Exhilarated by the frigid air, she practically floated along the dirt road, past the railway tracks, past the church, the town hall, and the school. She opened the iron gate and found the patch of fresh earth piled over her sister's body.

"Oh, Libby," she cried, dropping to her knees. "I didn't know. I didn't know . . ." She muttered unintelligible words and phrases, citing poems and prose she'd come across in her readings.

With nothing left to say, she managed to stand. A full moon pierced the night sky, pooling on the ground. She sloshed through the puddles of light along the path until it dipped downward into obscurity. There she came to an abrupt halt.

It was so large, she'd nearly missed it, nearly dismissed the lake of darkness as a mirage, a trick of the light. But it was no trick. Mounds of freshly turned earth were piled high behind an open hole in the ground. Her vision tunneled on the gaping black void. She stepped forward and stood on the precipice of the vast abyss that went down deeper than the moonlight could penetrate.

"Here I shall lie . . ." she sighed. "Until my skin has rotted and my bones are dust and my . . ."

Before she could finish her fever-induced ramblings, the earth quaked slightly. It was only a tiny tremor, but enough to throw Alice off kilter. The world tilted on its axis, and she slid down the embankment, the stones and sticks jabbing at her exposed skin as she fell. And before she reached the bottom, another tremor caused the earthen floor beneath her to give way, and she dropped further into a hole that she was certain would lead clear though to the other side of the world.

Once her body stopped moving and her senses settled, she discovered she was in a chamber of sorts beneath the pit. It was as though she'd stepped out of time, to a place where past and present mingled freely. It was strangely calm and quiet, then an earsplitting cry shattered the silence—something so unnatural, so unlike anything she had ever heard before.

Once the cry ended, there were a few seconds in which the only sound Alice could hear was the beating of her own heart. And then she saw it. It rose from the shadows, something unrecognizable, something horrible in shape and stature. It towered over her, its ghoulish head close to hers, its putrid stench filling the air around her.

Her fear was as sharp as a toothache. She hid her face in reflex and felt a sharp sting bite into her. Something sluggish in her veins was pushed aside, replaced by something slick and fast-moving. She swallowed her pain and fear, gobbled them up ravenously, and they turned to strength in her stomach and she was changed.

A gentle knock at the door drew Alice from her reverie, and in an instant, she was back in her room. Back in her bed.

"Alice," said Woodbridge Samuels. "It is time."

PART THREE

THE NAMELESS

Fear held Arlo in its icy grip. Cold beads of sweat formed on his brow. His chest rose and fell in jerky movements as he struggled for air.

He pressed his back harder against the jagged bark of the tree, stifling gasps with his hands. Little by little, his breathing slowed. He forgot all about what he'd been running from and focused now on what lay ahead.

Beyond him, down a slope, was an open space where no trees grew. In the glade stood a circle of bodies. Mist hovered over the dark ground, clotting at their feet, creating the illusion they were floating in both time and space.

The moonlight shone on their faces, and like the one-paddled moose, something wasn't right. Beneath their skin, veins glistened unnaturally. A clammy sense of wondrous dread filled Arlo as he took in the unnerving sight.

His first thought: It couldn't be real. It had to be a trick of the light. He blinked several times, covered his eyes with his hands, and rubbed hard, as if scrubbing away a stain that wouldn't come out. He looked again, but nothing had changed.

His second thought was of the comic book character Radioactive Man—only he emitted a greenish glow, and these people shone silver. At least they looked nothing like the angularly distorted bodies in *Zombie Army of Darkness*.

Among them, Arlo could make out the small figure of Hannah and the bowler-hatted head of the tall and lanky Woodbridge. He was sure he saw Alice and the twins, along with Martha and Malachi, Simon Sandborn, and the rest of the townsfolk he had met at the dinner celebration. He counted. They were all there. And more.

Leaning in, he heard muffled voices. He strained his ears but at first could not make out what they were saying. Perhaps this was some sort of ceremony and the glow could be attributed to a natural phenomenon. He tried desperately to convince himself of a rational explanation, but what he saw defied logic.

Arlo listened harder. He could hear the distant gurgle

of the river. It must be close. That was good. It meant the town wasn't far. Beyond the sound of rushing water, he picked out a smattering of words.

". . . no other way . . ."

". . . must be done . . ."

He struggled to make sense of what they were saying, but words scuttled here and there out of reach, like tiny insects into holes. The circle of bodies drew tighter, and the arguing voices grew louder.

". . . can't . . ."

". . . not yet . . ."

". . . not certain . . ."

The crowd broke into a furious roar. Everyone was speaking at once. Words overlapped in a tangle of hisses and vowels.

"If they should disappear . . ."

"People will search . . ."

"Get rid of them entirely . . ."

"Before it's too late . . ."

If they should disappear. Get rid of them entirely. The meaning flew like a steel arrow, piercing Arlo's heart. Just like the voices he had heard in the Samuels Mansion, they were talking about him, his mother, and Lola, and the meaning was nothing short of ominous.

As his brain scrambled to keep up, more thoughts

came to him, fast and furious. Did they know he had snuck out? Were they aware he was out here in the woods? Were they searching for him?

He wanted to bolt, but curiosity fastened his legs to the ground. Few trees stood between him and the clearing. In the cover of darkness, he stole from one trunk to the next, advancing slowly until he positioned himself behind a large oak and peered out around it.

From where he stood, the people had come fully into focus. Beneath the surface of their crepe-paper skin, patterns shone like shards of cracked glass. Like porcelain dolls that had been dropped and shattered.

". . . dangerous . . ."

". . . destroy us all . . ."

". . . must be settled . . ."

". . . tomorrow . . ."

One voice may have been Doc Brown. Another, possibly Martha Lovering or Hannah. Arlo couldn't be certain of either, but the last voice was Lovicia's. He'd have bet on it.

Arlo ducked behind the final trunk that stood between him and the clearing. But as he peered around it, a twig snapped beneath his feet and a face shot in his direction. His felt his skin crawl as milky white eyes bored straight into his. Then as quick as a cricket, Arlo was back behind the trunk.

The face had been Alice's. He was certain she had seen him.

His heart battered against his rib cage as he waited breathlessly. Five seconds . . . Ten seconds . . . His muscles tensed, preparing to dash. But there came no excited shouts of discovery. No earth-trampling patter of approaching footsteps. No rustling of leaves or snapping of twigs. Just the sound of the rushing water and the cloaked whispers of the townsfolk.

Arlo let out his breath. Alice hadn't seen him after all, or surely she'd have alerted the others. He was safe. For the moment.

Arlo's thoughts bounced like Ping-Pong balls. He should leave. Run back to the road as fast as he could. Head toward the last town they'd passed. But that would mean leaving his mother and sister behind.

A grapefruit-sized lump grew in his throat. No matter which way he spun the idea, running away wasn't an option. He couldn't leave his mother and Lola to save himself.

He resolved to go back. If no one had seen him, no one knew he'd been a silent witness to the strange event.

He had to return to his room, quickly, before they discovered he was gone.

Arlo took a single gingerly step backward. He moved slowly at first, one step at a time, forcing himself to remain calm and steady. He trod ever so lightly to make no sound, fighting the urge to turn and run wildly screaming. When he was certain he was out of earshot, he pivoted and tore in the opposite direction.

He didn't know where he was, but then he remembered the river. He paused and listened. He could hear the distant rush of water. If he followed the sound, he'd find his way to the bridge.

The farther Arlo got from the clearing, the quicker he moved. In order for his plan to work, he'd have to beat them back to the mansion. How much longer would they remain talking? How far was he from the covered bridge? Clearly, they'd be using the same one to cross the river. He had to get there first.

Arlo ducked and dodged as he scrambled through the woods, pausing only to listen. The sound of rushing water was getting louder.

At last, he found himself on the path not far from the bridge. He began to run as fast as his exhausted limbs could carry him. At the top of the slope, he looked right and then left. With no sign of the townspeople, he bolted down the hill.

In the distance, he heard a rasp of voices. The townsfolk must have taken a more direct route. They were close.

Though the wood creaked and moaned, he scrambled along the old timbers and out the other side of the bridge. He passed the tiny houses and made his way up the steep hill toward the Samuels Mansion. In his pocket was the phone, hopefully charging. But he couldn't risk taking it out. The light would give him away. He'd be caught before he got a signal.

The voices were right behind him now. They were through the bridge, most likely approaching Lovicia's house. Arlo broke into a full-blown sprint, his muscles burning, a stitch stabbing his side, but he didn't stop until he reached the front door.

Arlo turned the knob and stepped inside. Returning to the Samuels Mansion weighed on him. It felt heavy—like putting on an old winter coat you'd shed a season ago.

Arlo closed the door quietly, removed his sneakers, and crept up the stairs. He made it into his room just as the front door opened. He tore off his jacket and knit cap, flung them on the floor, and dove beneath the covers as a single set of footsteps reached the landing. They approached his room and paused outside his door.

He could feel a presence on the other side. Waiting. Listening. At last, footsteps retreated, and he heard a door open and close softly.

There was no question of restful sleep during the remaining hours of darkness. Although Arlo had squeezed his eyes shut to try to force sleep upon himself, he slipped in and out of consciousness. At last, he gave up, his stomach churning with unease, his mind raking over the events of the night.

He recalled in vivid detail the milky white eyes of the moose, of Alice, the earsplitting sound of the thing that had been stalking him, and the glistening silver patterns that shone beneath the skin of the townsfolk.

They hadn't looked like ghosts—not what Arlo imagined ghosts might look like, all wraithlike, wispy, and transparent—but rather like something unearthly. Alien.

At least for the moment, it appeared no one was aware of his nighttime prowling. Not even Alice. And more importantly, he had accomplished his goal: He had charged his phone.

His phone!

Arlo sat up abruptly, swung his legs over the edge of the bed, and reached for his jacket. He dug the piece of technology out of the pocket and hit the Home button. It burst into vibrant life.

His eyes darted to the tiny green icon of the battery in the top right corner. Fifty-five glorious percent. Now all he needed was a signal, and he'd be on his way out of Livermore.

Elated with his accomplishment, Arlo disconnected Lola's external charger and kissed it dramatically—it had served its purpose well but was no longer of any use to him. He buried it in his jacket pocket.

The screen on his phone announced half past eight in the morning. He could wait no longer. He opened his door, tiptoed past Alice's room, and proceeded toward his mother and Lola. He knocked gently. A wordless grumble invited him to enter.

Arlo's mother lay nestled beneath the covers half asleep while Lola sat cross-legged on the bed beside her.

"I've been up forever," Lola whispered. "Mom kept tossing and turning. I couldn't sleep."

His mother muttered something unintelligible and

then buried her head beneath her pillow. Her leg jutted out from the covers. The cast was beginning to crack. The flesh of her shin appeared darker than it had before. It could have been bruising, but Arlo worried infection was setting in.

"Me either," he sighed.

"Where did you get that?" asked Lola.

Arlo bristled. "What?"

"That sweatshirt," she said, gesturing toward his sleeve.

Arlo had forgotten all about his new clothing. He fabricated a quick lie. "I had it all along. I was wearing it under the other one. I put it on before we left the car. Don't you remember?"

Lola's expression pinched, as though she was straining to recall an event that eluded her.

He changed the subject. "Want to go for a walk?"

Her eyes lit. "Back to the owls?"

"Not the mill," he said stonily. "Let's walk to the church. And the school. Like we did the first day."

"Sure," she said, "I'll get Hannah."

"No!" Arlo protested louder than he'd meant. His mother stirred. "Let's go alone," he said softly, "just you and me."

"Fine. But I'm bringing Twiggy." She located the

strange root doll on the side table and held it gingerly. He gave a noncommittal sort of grunt and gestured for his sister to follow him out the door and down the hall.

The house was quiet, the silence so delicate Arlo was afraid it might bruise if he made a peep. He checked for signs of Alice, Woodbridge, and Mrs. Hawthorn, but thankfully no one was about. Arlo thought of the late-night gathering in the woods and shivered.

"You catching a cold?" asked Lola. "You don't look so good."

"I'm fine," said Arlo, raking his hands through his hair. The previous few nights were taking their toll. Carefully, he crept down the steps, urging Lola to tread lightly. In a moment they were in the foyer and out the door.

Something had happened in the short time between Arlo's late-night jaunt and the early morning hours. The temperature had dropped. The dew on the tree limbs and rooftops had frozen, covering the landscape in a gossamer film of silver.

Arlo's feet crunched as he walked over the gravel and frozen grass. His breath came out in plumes of white. A fine mist rained down, freezing in the air like tiny crystals.

"It's magical," said Lola. "Like we're in a snow globe and someone shook it."

Arlo tried to smile, but then he thought about the

ghastly images from the previous night and gave his head a shake. *If there's magic here*, he decided, *it's definitely the dark kind.*

He zipped up his jacket, took the wool cap from his pocket, and placed it on his sister. With purposeful strides, he plodded toward the spot just outside the mansion where he'd last caught a signal. The mist was transforming into snowflakes floating lightly to the ground. Glancing at the phone in his hand, Arlo sighed. Not one single bar materialized.

"What are you doing?" asked Lola, panting to keep up. "I thought your phone was dead."

"It was," he said, holding it up higher, as if that might possibly help.

"Then how's it charged?"

He had to fabricate another lie. "Your external charger. I took it before we left the car. When I took the sweatshirt."

She eyed him suspiciously. "Then why didn't you charge it yesterday or the day before?"

"I don't know," he said, frustration creeping into his tone. He walked here and there in a zigzag pattern, all the while eyeing the phone. No bars appeared. "In all the confusion, I guess I forgot about it. It's charged now. That's all that matters."

"All right," said Lola, with a burst of cheerfulness. "If you get a signal, we can call Dad . . ." She paused and then added, "Or maybe we should try Aunt Anita."

Arlo stopped walking and looked at his sister. Echoes of past disappointment filled the silence between them. Arlo nodded. If he got a signal, he'd try his aunt this time.

"Come on," he said. "Maybe we'll have some luck further up the road."

They crossed the railway tracks, past the fork in the road that led toward the mill. Veering right, they made their way toward the church and school. As he walked, Arlo was sucked into a sinkhole in his mind.

It was right after his mother's third treatment. The operation had been successful. His mother had remained optimistic and in good spirits from the very start. Arlo had tried his best to hold it together. They had gone for weeks and weeks pretending all was well, but then one day, in the flicker of an instant, the reality of the situation came crashing down on him.

Tears had prickled the back of his eyes, and his body began to quake. His mother, seeing his distress, held his hands tightly and looked into his eyes.

"It's going to be okay," she had said, her expression both helpless and resolute.

He'd wanted it to be true. Needed it to be true. And yet he couldn't bear to look at her. He had squeezed his eyes shut, sending spots flashing in his vision. He'd tried to pull away, but she'd held him firmly.

"It's going to be okay," she repeated, each word like an anchor, steadying him against the storm in his mind.

He opened his eyes and let the white dots dissipate. Was it? Was it really? She was making a promise she had no right to make, because Arlo knew it wasn't within her power to keep or break.

It's going to be okay.

Words so easily spoken, and yet, so often wrong.

His mother could see how tormented he was. How deeply her illness had affected him. It was then she had decided to send him to Dr. Lewis.

Arlo emerged from the haze of his thoughts to find himself standing in front of the graveyard. He sighed loudly. Now that he had plenty of battery life, he had zero reception. He wanted to smash the phone against a rock, but the only rocks in sight were tombstones.

An elaborately fashioned wrought-iron fence cordoned off the front and sides of the graveyard, forming a section separate from the rest of the landscape. The fence, covered in creeping ferns, their leaves now more gray than green, seemed to mark the place between the living and the dead. It was like a sort of barrier between worlds.

Through the twirling metalwork, Arlo could see a tangled mass of wild, overgrown grass and brush slowly being covered in flakes of fresh snow. He wondered for a moment if the fence was there to keep the living out. Or the dead in.

Before he could decide, Lola swept past him. She tried the handle, but the gate was locked, so she wound her hand through the intricate fretwork and clicked open the latch from the inside. The gate swung open, its hinges whining in protest.

"Look," she said, following the overgrown path toward a small slanted gravestone. She pointed to the name carved into its mossy face.

Arlo approached. "Mary Elizabeth Samuels."

"She must be related to Alice," said Lola. "Maybe it's her great great-great-grandma."

Arlo shook his head. "Look at the dates. Whoever Mary Elizabeth Samuels was, she couldn't be anyone's grandmother. She died when she was fourteen years old."

"That's not much older than you," said Lola.

Arlo gulped. It was bad enough seeing graves of old people, but seeing one of someone nearly his own age made it so much more frightening. "There was no medicine and stuff back then."

Talk of medicine made him think of his mother. Her leg hadn't looked good at all. If infection set in, it could spread quickly. He had to get a signal. He wandered further along the path that wound through the crumbling tombstones, down a slope, and away from the town, deeper and deeper into the overgrown brush.

It was snowing more heavily now. Their tracks were being covered, and Arlo's toes were getting numb. He wished he'd worn his boots. How silly he'd been for not taking them from the car. If he could just get a signal. He checked his phone. A bar flashed briefly, but then vanished again.

Lola scampered past. She didn't seem quite as affected by the cold. She disappeared through a mass of overgrown bushes and creepers that formed a tunnel over the path. Arlo ducked beneath it, and when he caught up to her, she was standing in front of a stone obelisk.

Beyond it was an enormous patch of earth that seemed slightly sunken compared to the rest of the landscape and where nothing grew. It was bleak and featureless. The woods closed in around it.

The monument, partially obscured by withered fern

fronds and winter greenery, had a large square base with several layers of squares on top, each progressively smaller. The final portion was a rectangular prism several feet tall that tapered to a pyramid point. Black moss grew thick on the crumbling gray stone.

Arlo glanced down at his phone. A single bar flickered in and out again. He looked up just as Lola was ripping off a strand of ivy that strangled the body of the stone. She brushed away flakes of snow to reveal a strange carving.

The image was startling. Arlo approached to get a better look. It was a crude etching depicting some kind of creature. It had blank stone eyes and a tangle of tentacle-like roots beneath its head. The head itself was formed of a totem of myriad smaller faces with bulbous eyes and mouths that telescoped outward, revealing tiny jagged teeth. It generated in Arlo's mind simultaneous images of an insect, a piece of rotting vegetation, and an ancient demon.

"Wow," he said, taken aback. "Who would erect an ugly memorial like this?" He crouched, and peering closer, he discovered an inscription. He ran a finger along the lettering and then read it aloud.

THAT IS NOT DEAD WHICH CAN ETERNAL LIE.

"What *is* it?" asked Lola. She held out her root doll. Turned upside down, it bore a striking resemblance to the face of the creature.

Before Arlo could respond, a familiar ping chimed. He looked down to discover his phone had two bars and an unread text message had popped up. It was from his father. Instinctively he pressed the icon.

Very funny, Arlo. Nearly fell for your little joke.

Arlo's mind spun with confusion. What did his father mean? What little joke? Before he knew what he was doing, his finger stabbed out his father's number, and the phone began to ring.

"Dad!" Arlo gasped. "Where are you? Are you on your way?"

"Very funny." The voice was soft and controlled, but there was an angry chill to the words. "You had me for a moment there. I nearly fell for it."

Arlo was confused. "What are you talking about? Why didn't you come get us like you said you would?"

There was a pause and a sigh, and then, "You really had me convinced. I'll give you that. I had the keys in my hand."

There was a faint whistling of the wind in the tall high trees, and out of the corner of his eye, Arlo thought he caught sight of a vague undulation in the woods beyond. His head snapped in the direction. He had a faint impression of a figure crouching at the base of a tree, hiding in its tangled roots. He startled and looked at Lola, hoping to direct her eyes toward it, but when he looked back again, there was nothing but bark and roots and grass. Whatever had dragged itself from the shadows was gone.

"I was about to drop everything and go running . . ." his father continued.

Arlo suppressed the urge to shout. Instead, he lowered his voice, and the words came out in a snakelike hiss. "Then why didn't you? I was counting on you."

"Look, Arlo," Dad replied. "I'm not falling for your mean-spirited attempt to lure me away on Thanksgiving weekend. I know you've been angry lately. With everything, with everyone—with me—but this is going too far. Sending me on a wild goose chase."

"Dad!" erupted Arlo, as much to stop the spinning of his own thoughts as the senseless ramblings of his father. "I have no idea what you're talking about. I don't have much time. If my battery dies again, I won't be able to contact you. I need you to come here. Come get us. We need to get out of Livermore!"

"Enough," His father was practically shouting, which he never did. He seemed to stop and place his anger in check, then added, "I Googled Livermore. It doesn't exist."

The world spiraled like an electrical vortex around

Arlo. "What?" It was the only word he managed, his voice a shadow of a whisper.

"The mill shut down in 1928, and the town was dissolved by the legislature. Its status was revoked." His father sounded exasperated now, as though he were stating something as obvious as the sky was blue.

"Wh-What are you saying?" Arlo's voice trembled as his brain scrambled to put meaning to his father's words.

"There is no Livermore, Arlo," his father huffed. "Hasn't been for about a century."

Waves of cold rippled through Arlo's body. He fought hard to hold himself upright. "Dad, please. I don't care what Google says. It's wrong. You have to believe me. You have to come. It's a life-or-death situation. I think Mom's leg is infected. She needs an antibiotic. Plus, the people here are strange. I can't explain."

"But, Arlo—"

"Please listen to me." He choked back his anger. His eyes pooled with tears. He blinked them away. "I've never lied to you. I'm telling the truth."

There was a long pause at the other end. A twig snapped. Something moved again. Arlo was certain he caught sight of a shadow slipping behind a large trunk. He suddenly realized how isolated and cold and alone he felt.

"Please," he said softly, "I need you."

His father sighed. "Okay, okay . . ." He sounded less convinced, more worn down. "But if you say the town exists and Google says it doesn't, how do I find you?"

Arlo's thoughts scrambled. They had been on Route 302 at one point, he recalled, then Route 112, then the dirt roads . . .

"The water park," he said suddenly. "Splish! Splash! Find the water park. We drove past it and then a campground. If you find those, stay on the same road until you get to railroad tracks, then veer left at the fork. Keep going. You'll find the car wreck. Wait for us there. We will be there. Just promise you'll come."

There was a pause that lasted an eternity, and Arlo worried his battery might drain before his father would respond. He held his breath and said a silent prayer, and it must have worked because his father let out a long whistle through his teeth and then said, "If I leave now, it will be dark and cold by the time I arrive. Can you stay put one more night?"

Relief washed over Arlo. He was so thrilled his father was agreeing to come, he muttered affirmations.

"I'll leave before dawn. I'll find the car and wait for you there."

"We'll be there!" Arlo croaked out several thank-yous, clicked End, and stared at his phone.

"What was all that about?" said Lola.

"Nothing. Just Dad being Dad," said Arlo, but he didn't look at her. He was eyeing the black trunks of trees beyond the stone monument. He might have imagined the movement. It was possible, but his gut told him otherwise.

The phone's battery was at thirty percent. It was draining quicker than usual. He was so relieved his father had agreed to come. He'd find the water park and the car, and they'd find him.

But what he had said puzzled Arlo. Despite his low battery, Arlo pulled his gaze from the trees. He couldn't resist the urge to check while he still had a signal.

He opened the map app, entered the town name, and watched the circle spin. There was a Livermore in California and a Livermore Falls in Maine, but no Livermore, New Hampshire.

"Did you lose the signal?" asked Lola.

"No. Just can't seem to bring Livermore up on Google Maps."

"Probably just a glitch," said Lola. "Maybe you just need to run an update."

He didn't think that was it at all, but he didn't want to alarm her. "Yeah. I'm sure you're right."

He opened his browser. Before he could enter the name of the town, someone approached from behind.

"What are you doing?"

Arlo jumped.

In the light of day, Hannah appeared exceedingly ordinary. There wasn't anything the least unusual or fantastic about her. Seeing her now, up close, it was hard to reconcile this face with the one he'd witnessed the night before. His panicked certainty wavered and diminished, leaving him feeling confused and slightly foolish.

Could he have been mistaken? Could it have been a trick of the moonlight? It was possible, and yet, he could not shake the ghoulish image from his mind's eye. He resisted the urge to reach out and touch her.

"Hannah!" said Lola, leaving the stone monument and running up to the girl. She took her friend's hand warmly. "Arlo got a signal. He talked to our dad. He's not coming until tomorrow. That means we have another day together!"

Hannah's eyes widened. "A signal? I thought your phone had died?"

Despite the normalcy of her face, its bland features, there was a cleverness in her expression he'd only just noticed.

"He used my external charger. He forgot he had it, right, Arlo?"

Hannah stared at Arlo, her eyes glistening with an intensity that made him uneasy. He had the strangest sensation, like fingers poking and probing inside his mind. He needed to deflect her attention. His eyes whirled around and settled on the monument. "Who's buried there?"

Hannah followed his gaze. She regarded the monument thoughtfully for a moment. "No one," she said flatly. "We call it the shadow grave."

"The what?" asked Lola.

"The shadow grave." She smiled. "Because it's empty. No bodies."

A slow shiver curled up Arlo's spine. He had never heard the term *shadow grave* before, and he couldn't help but wonder what bodies this one awaited.

Lola approached the monument. "What's this ugly thing?" She ran a finger along the image of the grotesque creature. "And what's this inscription mean?"

Hannah shrugged. "I'm not sure. I think it means people don't really die. Our spirits live on."

She turned abruptly, took Lola by the hand, and pelted back up the path toward the town, crying out, "Follow me! There's snow! We can go sledding!" The two girls' giggles echoed after them.

Arlo stared at the shadow grave. All of a sudden, he had a violent desire to get out of the graveyard and back into the open air. He retraced his steps, following Hannah and Lola toward the Samuels Mansion.

He would tell his mother about his phone call. He'd tell her his father would come this time—he was certain of it. But he wouldn't tell her what his father had said about the town. It didn't matter. Soon he'd be out of Livermore. Soon the whole weekend would be nothing more than a memory.

18

"He's coming," said Arlo. He had waited patiently by his mother's bedside, careful not to disturb her until she woke. "I was able to charge the phone—don't ask—and get a signal, and Dad is coming."

She raised an eyebrow and a paper-thin smile spread mockingly across her lips.

"No. Really," he insisted. "This time he is. At least, he promised."

His mother sat up with a groan. Arlo could tell she was in pain by the way she moved her leg. She adjusted the bathrobe and cinched the belt tighter around her waist.

"Like the time he promised to take you to the zoo? Or the time he promised to sharpen those skates? Or the time—"

"I know. I know," Arlo interrupted, frustrated she was making him relive moments he'd rather forget. "I'm not making excuses for him anymore. But"—he paused for a moment, wondering if he was deluding himself yet again—"this is different."

The girls had come tumbling inside the mansion shouting for mittens and scarves, drawing all the attention from Mrs. Hawthorn and Woodbridge with their talk of snow and sledding. Arlo had managed to slip upstairs virtually unnoticed. Only Alice had stood in the far corner of the room staring up at him, her face stiff and expressionless as he headed to his mother's room.

"He's coming," he said. "Tomorrow morning. I told him where to find the car. He's leaving really early. Before dawn. We'll meet him at the car."

His mother sighed, and he couldn't tell if it was out of pain, exhaustion, frustration, or something entirely different. He'd rather be leaving Livermore this very minute, but realistically—especially now with the snow—they wouldn't get far without a ride waiting. One more day, he told himself. One more night, and they'd be on their way.

"Where's Lola?" she asked, as if only now realizing she wasn't in the room with them.

"Sledding."

"*What?*"

"It's past noon. You've been asleep all morning," he said. "It's been snowing. She and Hannah had a quick bite and then bundled up in coats and scarves and went sledding down the hill with some of the other kids."

"Really?" she said, raking a hand through the jagged patches of hair. "Well, sounds like fun." She looked paler than the night before—that plus the sagging cast made Arlo's heart thud slightly in his chest.

"Yeah. She's having a great time." He tried to sound cheerful. The last word stretched into a cavernous yawn. He was so tired after his sleepless night. He needed rest. Badly. Instead he found himself saying, "I'm starving. Let's get some lunch and then you can go out for a while and watch them. It's not like there's anything else to do around here."

"Sure," she said. "Sounds like a . . ." She stopped midsentence. "Wait . . ."

He was halfway to the door when he halted and turned to face her. She stared at him for a moment. A shadow stole across her face. It reminded him of the sky before a storm—all dark and ominous and threatening.

"Sit down," she said. She patted the mattress beside her. He resisted, but she drew him gently, imperceptibly toward her, as though reeling him in with an invisible line. He lowered himself, and she placed an arm around his shoulders.

"There's something I've been meaning to tell you." Her voice was low and soft. She fidgeted with her fingers, the broken, jagged nail starkly out of place among periwinkle talons. "It's the reason I brought you on this trip, the reason I wanted some time away from everything and everyone—"

Arlo's mouth went chalk-dry. This could end a million different ways, but there was only one he dreaded beyond imagination. Thankfully, before she had a chance to continue, there came a sharp knock at the door.

"Lunchtime," said Mrs. Hawthorn. "Your presence is requested in the dining room."

Arlo sprang to his feet. He'd never welcomed an interruption more in his life. His mother tried to protest, to pull him back, but he wriggled from her grasp.

"I'm starving. And you have to eat—keep up your strength. We have to hike back to the car tomorrow morning. Once we get to the car, everything will be okay. Everything."

He continued to babble, placing more words and distance between them. He had to keep talking to prevent her from saying what he was terrified to hear.

"You heard Mrs. Hawthorn—*our presence has been requested*. We can't keep these people waiting. We can't insult them. Who knows what they're liable to do? I'll wait for you in the hall while you get dressed."

He slipped outside and closed the door behind him before she could get a single word out. In the hall, he shifted side to side. He had to stop his mind from wandering to dark places he'd have trouble escaping.

A portrait on the wall snagged his attention. It might have been considered decorative but for its bleakness. It was a black-and-white photograph of a pale young girl wearing a light-colored dress with a dark satin sash and a high lace collar buttoned to the top. She was seated in a large chair, her hands folded neatly, one over the other, in her lap.

He leaned in close and studied the girl's face, and suddenly it hit him—what was strange about some of the faded portraits he'd seen hanging on the walls—the people in these portraits, their eyes were shut. Given the faded, black-and-white nature of the photographs, it almost made them look as though they had no eyes.

"No digital cameras or Photoshop in those days," he

muttered to himself. He thought of all the silly filters Lola used. She'd give herself dramatic makeup, crazy hairstyles, googly eyes, cat whiskers, even a narwhal horn.

A name and date were scrawled across the bottom of the photograph. It gave him a sharp jolt. It was the same name and date he'd seen on the gravestone. Mary Elizabeth Samuels. 1880.

"It's a memento mori," said Alice. She had come upon him silently and was regarding the photograph alongside him.

"What's that?" asked Arlo, afraid of the answer.

"A photograph taken shortly after death—a way of honoring and remembering the dead."

A souvenir of the dead. The idea sent shivers parading up Arlo's spine, but by her expression, it was plain Alice did not mind the subject. In fact, there was almost a kind of longing in her tone that suggested she enjoyed the topic.

"Mortality rates were high in those days," she continued. "Child deaths were particularly common."

"Interesting," he said in a way that implied something entirely different. He pointed to the name and date. "So, this girl, Mary, she was dead when the photo was taken."

"No." Alice shook her head. "Not quite. It was taken before her face was ravaged."

"Huh?"

"By smallpox."

Arlo nodded. He'd heard of smallpox. The disease was long gone, but apparently laboratories in the US and Russia still stored the virus. He knew all this because *Zombie Army of Darkness* was based on a mutated smallpox virus that had escaped a laboratory and had decimated the human population, turning them into zombies.

"She was a relative of yours?" he asked. But before he could probe further, his mother stepped into the hall, suspending the morbid conversation.

"Hello, Alice," she said. "I thought you'd be sledding with the girls."

Alice turned her attention from Arlo and the portrait, her expression once again flat and unreadable, as though someone had drawn a blind down. "I don't care much for the cold."

"Then will you have some lunch with us?" his mother asked.

Arlo willed Alice to say no. He wanted to search the study—especially now that he'd seen the gravestone and the portrait of Mary Samuels. Something bothered him—though he couldn't quite put his finger on what it was.

He was desperate for a peek at the town registry. He was sure Alice would get in the way, but unfortunately, she'd become something akin to gum stuck to the bottom of his shoe—annoying and difficult to get rid of.

"Of course," said Alice, much to Arlo's dismay. "Follow me."

"You two go ahead," he said quickly. "I'll meet you there." He grinned a little too wide, detecting a hint of suspicion on both of their faces. But when his mother shrugged and turned, so did Alice. The two descended the stairs, turned a corner, and were out of sight.

He had to move quickly if he hoped to locate the study, snoop around a bit, and make it to the dining room in good time. When he was sure they were out of sight, he tiptoed down the steps and headed in the opposite direction, down a long hall he'd taken the first night.

The house was a veritable maze of corridors. He looped in one direction, then another, passing rooms he was certain he'd passed previously. He tried several doors.

There was a parlor, a cloakroom, a conservatory, a drawing room, and even an armory filled with old-fashioned gun racks and antlers hanging on the walls.

He imagined ribbons of blue smoke and low rumbling voices—bodies slouched in the deep leather chairs now cracked with time.

He had nearly given up when he tried one last door and discovered the dusty study. He inhaled the musky scent of yellowing paper.

With his heart beating in his throat, he made a beeline for the desk and the town registry. He snatched up the book and tore open the drapes to banish the darkness.

The book was heavier than he'd expected. He ran a hand over the cracked reddish-brown leather, feeling his fingers rise and dip over the deep grooves of the lettering. With a sense of trepidation, he creaked open the spine, and a plume of dust exploded into the air. He rubbed his nose to stifle a sneeze and then began to read.

Vital Records Relating to Births,
Marriages, and Deaths
Registry Department, Town of Livermore

The words were handwritten, as if by a quill or fountain pen, with embellished capitals and curly flourishes. The ink was faded, the script so fancy it was difficult to read. Arlo turned the goose-fat-colored page, and flecks of dust danced like glitter where they caught the light. He fanned the air and continued.

July 11, 1876

Upon completion of the mill and by the authority of the state of New Hampshire, the town of Livermore, formerly known as Elkins Grant, has been incorporated, encompassing 80,000 acres of land, ten miles long and twelve miles wide in the Pemigewasset wilderness.

July 11, 1876

First town meeting held, officiated by Charles Murphy and Ben Sullivan. Census taken. The following is a list of those residing at present in and about the township.

Arlo skimmed the page. His eyes brushed the list of names and became ensnared. A tightening knot of wrongness wrenched inside his belly. It yanked tighter, tauter, until it squeezed panic up his throat. He turned page after page.

Before he could make sense of it, he heard footsteps in the hall. They were soft, but growing louder, and they were heading right for the study. He looked right, then left, but there was nowhere to hide, so he stood immobile, caught like a fly in solid amber, as Alice entered the room. It was uncanny, like she had a tracking device on him.

Arlo felt the jolt of impact as her eyes locked with his. The air in the room felt suddenly different, as though it were thinner and cooler. He and Alice were glued or, more likely, frozen to the very spots where they stood.

She glanced at the book in his hand, and then at the stack of old picture frames in the corner of the room before returning her gaze to his. She appeared paler—if that were even possible—peering into his eyes like he had a secret hidden there.

Arlo was trapped. He wanted to move forward or backward. He wanted to escape, but he'd forgotten how his body worked.

At last, she made a move. She walked to the pile of picture frames, found one, and held it out for him to see. "It's time you know the truth."

"It was all my fault," Alice said.

Arlo's eyes were fastened to the picture in her hands. It was a family portrait with a mother, father, and two children. The mother sat in a Victorian armchair. She wore a long lace dress that reached her ankles. It had a high collar and billowing sleeves. The girls were young—one an infant, the other a toddler. The baby sat perched on its mother's lap, while the older child stood, barely reaching the mother's knee. In the background, the father loomed, tall and lean, the line of his brow so heavy it plunged his eyes into shadow.

"If only . . . If only I—" she continued, but her words were cut short by the clip-clop of several pairs of footsteps converging in the hall just outside the door.

Alice's eyes grew wide, and she placed a finger to her

lips. Arlo clamped his mouth and held his breath. He could feel every hair on the back of his neck stand on end.

"Alice is keeping an eye on the boy," said the voice of Mrs. Hawthorn. "Hannah and the twins are with the sister."

Arlo's gaze was fixed on Alice's. Her expression was somber but unreadable, as though the blind had fallen once again.

"He managed to charge the phone," said the unmistakable trill of Martha Lovering. "He's reached the father."

"It cannot wait," said Woodbridge.

"It must be done . . ." said Mrs. Hawthorn.

"Yes," said Martha.

The footsteps headed off in different directions. When all was silent, Alice leaned in conspiratorially. "I will tell you everything, I promise," she whispered. "But not here. There are eyes and ears in these walls."

Arlo resisted the urge to search for disembodied eyeballs and earlobes dangling from the ceiling. Instead, he observed Alice intently. Her large brown eyes were wide and fixed so firmly, so unwaveringly on his it made him squirm. He had a sudden flashback to the night before, when he had seen them in the moonlight glowing pearly-white. He shuddered.

She had been instructed to keep an eye on him, which was exactly what she was doing. And yet, she had kept their presence in the study a secret. Why wouldn't she have exposed him? She promised to tell him everything. Why would she do that? Was she trying to win his trust only to betray him later? Try as he might, he could not discern her motives.

"Follow me to the dining room," she said. "We'll eat lunch, and then you'll agree to go sledding. Once outside, we'll find a place to talk. Privately."

Arlo did not move. He didn't trust Alice, but he also didn't think he had much choice. He'd read spy novels where double agents pretended to work for one side, all the while conspiring with the other. If Alice was a double agent, he'd be one too. He'd pretend to trust her. He'd go along with what she said. For now.

There was a scene in *Zombie Army of Darkness* when the Leftovers—those unaffected by the virus—wanted to rush out and meet the Zombie Army head-on, but one of them, Dr. Zoid, convinced the group to hide and conduct covert operations to discover as much as they could about the Zombies and their weaknesses first.

Knowledge is power, Zoid says. *And right now, they know more about us than we do about them.*

There were things Arlo had seen, things he knew, and

things he suspected. But the townspeople knew more about him, which gave them power. He needed Alice to fill in the gaps—assuming she'd tell the truth—so he'd have a clear picture of what he was up against.

He nodded, giving her the impression he trusted her. Her arm clamped to his sleeve, and together, they slipped out of the study, through the maze of halls, and into the dining room.

"What took you so long?" asked his mother as they approached. "I've already finished."

Arlo eyed Alice.

"He got lost," she said.

Arlo's mother narrowed her eyes but didn't press further.

Lunch was a painful exercise in restraint. Arlo sat stiffly, responding to his mother's questions and comments with a nod, a shrug, a word or two. He tried hard not to meet Mrs. Hawthorn's eyes as she dished out bowls of thick soup and hard lumps of homemade bread.

He ate with great concentration while observing Alice covertly. Once, he could have sworn he saw her hold Mrs. Hawthorn's gaze a little too long. A wordless communication seemed to pass between them, flowing like an electrical current from one to the other. He wondered what the message might have been.

Then Alice smiled—a small, thoughtful sort of smile. She leaned forward across the table, and Arlo could see flecks of gold in her dark eyes. "Should we join the others and go sledding?"

"Great idea," said his mother, nudging him. Mrs. Hawthorn had poured her a cup of tea. "Go on. It'll be fun."

"Um . . . sure," Arlo found himself saying, though it occurred to him her words—*I will tell you everything, I promise*—might be nothing more than wriggling worms baiting a hook. Was he a foolish cod tricked by a shiny lure?

"Want to come out and watch?" he asked his mother.

"Not now," she said. "I think I need to lie down again." She looked suddenly tired and pale. "But you go and have fun."

Alice stood. "Come on."

In the foyer, Arlo pushed his feet into his sneakers, still damp from his previous trek in the snow. He accepted the wool mittens and cap offered to him—they had an unpleasant damp-dog odor—zipped up his jacket, and stepped out into the chilly afternoon.

"Eeeee!" shouted Lola, as her wooden sled zipped down the hill. The twins were at the bottom already.

Hannah looked on, clapping with excitement. Seeing

Alice and Arlo, she waved them over. Alice and Arlo watched for a while as Lola, Hannah, the twins, and a few of the other kids took turns careening down the sheet of snow.

"We're having the best time!" said Lola, galumphing up the hill, sled in tow.

Hannah took Alice by the hand and added. "Let's make their last day enjoyable."

Their last day. Arlo gulped. He didn't like the sound of that.

"We will," said Alice, assuring her with a firm grip, then pulling her hand free. "We're going for a walk now. Arlo wants to see the schoolhouse one last time."

One last time. Again, Arlo had a strange sense of foreboding. A terrible feeling these phrases were not coincidental.

"Um, yeah," he said.

"We'll come, too!" said Lola, handing the sled to one of the boys.

"No," said Arlo. "You stay here. We'll be back soon."

Lola stopped. She looked at Arlo, then Alice. Hannah leaned in and whispered something in her ear, which made her giggle and sent a burst of red flames into Arlo's cheeks.

He wanted to say, *No! No! It's not that!* But then he'd

risk Lola and Hannah tagging along. Instead, he inhaled sharply, scowled, and said to Alice, "Let's go."

"Wait!" said Lola. She withdrew the doll from her pocket. "Hold on to Twiggy for me while I toboggan. Keep her safe. Promise."

Arlo rolled his eyes. He took the ugly thing and tucked it into his jacket pocket. He glanced at Alice and sighed.

Sensing his embarrassment, Alice kept a good distance as they walked across the railroad tracks in the direction of the schoolhouse. The awkwardness persisted as they meandered past the church, Alice giving a brief account of its construction, then the town hall—recounting events that had taken place there, and finally even the schoolhouse, which she said she hadn't entered in years.

He'd tried to question her, but Alice did not answer. Instead, she took the lead, heading straight for the graveyard.

There, she halted outside the wrought-iron gate. She regarded him with a dreamy, wistful expression. "Graveyards are places for the living—not the dead."

Cold crept in through the soles in his sneakers. "What do you mean?"

"All the statues and headstones," she said, gesturing

with a theatrical air, "they're for the living, not the dead. The living try to hold on, but the dead don't want to be held. The dead want to leave." She slipped her small hand through the fretwork just as Lola had done, undid the latch, and swung open the creaky gate.

Arlo pondered this as she led him along the path, deeper and deeper into the graveyard. He had walked this path earlier today. He could see his footprints still fresh in the snow. He knew where they were headed, and despite a warning thudding in his heart, he followed her until they arrived at the base of the strange monument. At the shadow grave.

There she stopped and gazed about, as if to make certain no one was near. Through tendrils of weeping willows came a melancholic whistle of wind as she ran a hand along the image of the bizarre-looking beast carved into the face of the obelisk.

"The image is inaccurate," she said, her words warbling like creek water around reeds and stones. "It was added decades later. Most couldn't recall the details, they'd been so frightened, others too clouded with the delirium of fever."

He swallowed. "What is it?"

Alice eyed him intently, her pupils like black holes drawing him into their gravitational pull. "You can't understand a tiny part of a picture—one single piece of a puzzle—without first seeing the whole."

Her voice slipped away momentarily. Then she inhaled, a deep breath before a plunge, and began again. This time she spoke resolutely, quickly, words tumbling from her lips in torrents until they became an endless, gasping stream Arlo could barely process fast enough.

She told him about her sister, Libby's, illness. How everyone, including her mother and father, had forgotten all about Alice's birthday. She described the beautiful dress and the glorious party Libby had received on her twelfth birthday. She explained how she had snuck into her sister's room to retrieve the dress, how she had paraded all around town, making sure everyone saw her and congratulated her. And then, how the fever came. The dress they had clothed Libby in to take her final photograph—the memento mori—contained the virus. It had infected everyone Alice had come into contact with.

Sorrow draped like a veil over her eyes, and she shuddered slightly. "I overheard Father, Doc Brown, and Simon Sandborn. They had dug an enormous pit. We were all to be buried—alive if necessary—to stop the spread."

She stretched out her hands over the expanse of land

beyond the monument. "This was it. This was the spot." She contemplated it for a moment, then continued. "I came here at night. The pit was deep and dark. The grave had to be excavated before the ground became too cold and too hard. Before they'd be too weary with disease, too incapacitated to dig. It had to be large enough and deep enough to fit us all."

Arlo's eyes grew wide. He couldn't believe what he was hearing.

"The earth gave way, and I slipped down the side into the dirt bottom. Then the ground opened up further, and I was swallowed. That's when I saw it. Something had been unearthed. Something that ought not to have been disturbed. Something that had been here long before we had. Possibly long before humans had populated the planet, before the age of dinosaurs even."

The breath caught in Arlo's throat. "Wha-What is it?"

"No one knows." Alice bit her lip. "We call it the Nameless."

She pronounced these last words with complete detachment—no intonation, no pitch, no inflection—as though they were words from some ancient language she had never quite learned to speak.

Spiders crawled up Arlo's spine. He had listened, wide-eyed, mouth gaping, to everything Alice had said.

And like the sun peeking over the horizon, everything that had previously been vague and abstract in the shadowy confusion of his mind was suddenly clear, transformed into a structure that, in a warped way, made sense.

The portrait.

The shadow grave.

The Nameless.

Part of his brain resisted as he struggled to come to terms with the sheer amazement of what she was saying. And yet, he couldn't deny the world was a far stranger and more mysterious and complicated place than anyone could imagine. It was full of things science could not even begin to explain.

Arlo had read the town registry. He had seen the names of people such as Mary Elizabeth Samuels—Libby—who had lived and died over a century ago. But there were other names, such as Alice, Lovicia, Simon Sandborn, and Martha Lovering. These had birth dates but no records of death.

Alice kept talking. Arlo watched her lips move, make sounds; her pupils were black and dilated, her cheeks hollow and sunken, and suddenly she reminded him of a Picasso painting, distorted and tilted.

"It pierced me—or perhaps bit me—I can't really say

which," she said. "I felt a tingling that quickly became a searing in the underside of my skin. It was as though something had infected my body, something so excruciating—I could barely stand it. But then, all at once, it settled, and I felt strangely calm and comfortable. No longer afraid. No longer ill."

Arlo pictured something entering Alice's bloodstream, and he was suddenly reminded of an experiment his teacher had done once in science class. She'd cooled a plastic bottle of water in a pail of ice and salt for ten minutes. The water in the bottle was still liquid, but when she struck it sharply against her desk, crystals formed near the top, moving swiftly downward until the water froze completely in an instant.

"So . . . this . . . procedure . . . cured you?" said Arlo.

"That's what I thought." A look of deep sadness filled her eyes. "So I brought all the others to the Nameless in order to fix my mistake and to help cure them as well. And at first we really believed we were cured. But then time passed, and all who hadn't been changed grew old. They withered and died, but we—the changed ones—continued to live unaffected by the passage of time."

Alice had been talking so quickly, so desperately, and then all at once, her momentum slowed. "We have learned to keep ourselves isolated. People are cruel to those who are different. To that which they don't understand."

It suddenly all made sense to Arlo. As crazy and wild and fantastical as it was, it somehow all made sense. A breeze blew the ends of Alice's hair. They fluttered, and Arlo thought he caught sight of something—a faint abnormality in the skin along the side of her neck. A distinctive circular mark.

"You have put yourself in danger by coming here," she continued. Her voice became choppy. Fluency abandoned her. The words now fell from her lips like stones. "There are those who would keep you and those who would get rid of you, and as of yet, they are undecided. There is another meeting tonight—and whichever way it goes, it will not end well."

The snow was falling again. It was late afternoon. There would be only another two or three hours of daylight. Arlo shivered and hugged his arms to his chest.

Questions bounced around inside his skull, crashing into one another, multiplying with each impact. Could it really be true? Were they in danger? Where was the Nameless now?

As if in response, he thought he felt the tiniest of tremors beneath his feet. The ground shifted as though something buried beneath the earth had awoken. He imagined he smelled something dank, like earth dug up and hitting air for the first time in eons. He recognized this odor from last night.

He couldn't stay a moment longer. He had to get out. He had to get his sister and his mother and leave Livermore. He pivoted and scrambled as quickly as his cold limbs could carry him back toward the gate.

"Wait!" Alice called. "There's something else! Something you need to know!"

But Arlo had heard enough. He bolted up the path, out of the graveyard toward the mansion. He staggered as though the ground below him were uneven and shifting. Like he was running through a carnival fun house. Behind him he could hear Alice calling, "Wait!"

There was nothing else she could tell him that would make him want to leave quicker than he already did. All he needed now was to get to his mother and sister. He'd have to get them to believe what he barely believed himself in order to move quickly, secretly, without help or shelter awaiting them.

He made it to the top of the hill far ahead of Alice. Hannah seemed to search for her and then stare at him questioningly, but Lola drew her attention. She ran with the sled and then belly flopped onto it, zipping down the hill. The sled lurched sideways and tipped. Lola rolled several feet before coming to a crumpled heap, her giggles resonating in the air around her.

Arlo raced to the bottom of the hill. He picked up the sled, and she got up and came running to grab it. "Looks like you're having fun."

"The best!" said Lola. She reached for the sled, but he held on to it.

"It's cold." He tried to sound casual, though his heart was beating in his throat. "Come inside and warm up. You must be freezing."

"Nope," she said. "Not yet. I'm not even cold." She snatched the sled from his grasp.

Arlo wanted to say something. He wanted to tell her all that he knew, but how would he begin? How would he explain? And with Hannah and the twins looking on, it wasn't possible.

"We need to check on Mom," he said.

"But—"

"Now," he said, taking her by her gloved hand and practically dragging her toward the top of the hill. "Mom is waiting."

"I have to go inside now," said Lola, scowling at Arlo and handing the sled to Hannah. "This was so much fun."

"I'll meet you in a while . . . for dinner?" suggested Hannah. Lola grinned and nodded.

Arlo was at the porch. He held the door open for Lola, and she stepped inside. Alice had caught up and stood beside Hannah and the boys. She stared at Arlo as though she had more to say.

20

Arlo burst into his mother's room, dragging Lola, who protested angrily for having been made to leave all the fun.

"I have to tell you something," he said urgently.

His mother was lying on the bed. She looked solemn, her eyes slightly glazed. "I have something to tell you, too."

Arlo danced frantically. "This is important. You have to listen." He held Lola's hand. "Both of you."

"My one-year appointment . . ." his mother said softly. She turned to face them. "It's Monday."

Arlo let go of Lola, and at once the room tilted. All the frenetic energy he'd felt a moment ago drained from him like water through a sieve. He stopped moving. The world, as he knew it, was sinking.

"It's why I wanted to go away this weekend . . ."

Her voice seemed to be coming from a great distance, soft against the buzzing and ringing in Arlo's mind. The reservoir of hope he'd been sandbagging sprang a leak. Its contents pooled on the floor, black and murky, threatening to drown him.

". . . so we could be alone—the three of us—and I could tell you. I'm sure I'm fine, but there's a chance it might be—"

"Back," said Arlo. The word came out of him choked and dry.

His mother had once told him emotions had scents. They had flavors and textures. And some, like fear, were complex recipes containing many ingredients: sorrow, anger, hopelessness . . . The concoction bubbled in Arlo's stomach, making him queasy.

He knew he should be doing what Lola was doing. He should be throwing himself at his mother, hugging her tightly, burying his head in her shoulder, but instead, he just stood there.

It was over. All behind them. His mother had battled and won. Why should she have to go through the worry all over again? It wasn't right. It wasn't fair.

"So, the appointment is Monday," repeated his mother with muted cheer.

Lola listened quietly, intently, to all she had to say, but Arlo was now a million miles away, lost in clouds of gray mist swirling inside his brain. He pictured his mother sitting in the hospital, medicine trickling into her veins. And then, for a brief stabbing moment, another image flashed before his eyes—an image of the hideous monster carved into the obelisk. Of Alice. Of the townspeople. Of the moonlight refracted into a million shards beneath their skin, making them glow like angels.

The gray fog in Arlo's brain dissipated as a single solid thought pierced the haze and etched itself into the air before him in bold black capitals: *WHAT IF* . . .

"We're hoping for the best, but just in case . . ." his mother was saying staunchly. Resolutely.

No one spoke for a long time. But like a bird pecking at Arlo's brain, the thought continued to tap a steady rhythm.

What if . . .

What if . . .

He moved to the window and glanced out at the forest covered in freshly fallen snow. Soon it would be dark. It got dark so early here. The thing about being in the middle of nowhere—isolated, secluded—was there was nothing anchoring him in place and time. For all he knew, a hundred years had passed since they'd arrived in Livermore.

A thousand.

As Lola and his mother talked softly, Arlo abandoned himself to a sorrow so deep it was cavernous. He closed his eyes and let himself fall, dropping into darkness. He thought he might fall forever—and perhaps he had—but then those sharp, jagged words snagged him.

What if . . .

What if . . .

He managed to pull himself from the abyss of his thoughts and open his eyes. He turned to face his mother and Lola. His voice came out in a reedy whisper.

"What if . . ."

The idea was so wild. So unbelievable. He cleared his throat and began again. "What if . . ."

His mother stared at him with veiled curiosity. She smiled a tiny crooked smile. A smile full of sadness and fatigue. He frowned hard. How would he get her and Lola to understand? To believe?

He started again, gently, carefully, each syllable distinct, as though his words were barbed and might catch in his throat. "I watched a program on invasive species last year. It was about a tree-killing bug called the emerald ash borer. Do you know how the ash borer survives the winter?"

For a moment, his mother looked at him quizzically, as if he were a stranger and she was trying to decide what it was about him she recognized. And then recognition seemed to flood back into her eyes, and along with it came a kind of pity.

"Why are you talking about bugs?" snapped Lola, confused and annoyed.

He ignored his sister and continued. "In winter, the ash borer can survive freezing temperatures by entering a state of diapause. It's like a state of suspended animation. It doesn't get older. It doesn't develop. It just lies there under the bark of the tree, waiting for spring to bring it back to life."

"Like hibernation," muttered his mother.

"No." He shook his head. "It's not sleeping. It's like they're semifrozen."

"Like the iguanas," said Lola.

"Yes," said Arlo. "Yes, like the iguanas. And wood frogs. And wooly bear caterpillars—they actually freeze. Ice forms in their bodies. They're like little statues. For centuries, scientists have known that some creatures can survive being frozen, but they still don't know the magic behind it. Not exactly."

He looked at his mother and waited, but she didn't

speak. Her smile was gone now. A small frown creased her brow like she was thinking really hard. Like she was trying to understand where he was headed with this.

"And there are tardigrades—water bears," he said hurriedly, "these micro animals that can enter a state of cryptobiosis, totally suspending their metabolism, going without food or water for more than thirty years. They can survive just about anything. Extreme temperatures, pressure, dehydration, radiation. They can survive under ice, on top of volcanoes, and even in the vacuum of space."

Arlo could feel an excited, almost crazed look emanating from his eyes. Lola stared at him as though he had grown a second head, as though he were something strange and to be feared, but he persisted.

"There are things in nature—things scientists don't fully understand. It's a kind of *magic*."

He used the word a second time for emphasis, to prove that there was, in fact, magic in the world, magic even scientists couldn't explain.

"I need you to remember all this, because I'm about to tell you something strange. Something that will sound weird and fantastical."

He dropped to his knees beside the bed. He took his

mother's hands in his as though to beg her to listen. "I know this is going to sound incredible. Unbelievable. But you have to listen. Promise you'll listen."

He tried hard to make his voice sound more level, more calm, more reasonable than he felt, but then the room suddenly overflowed with his voice, syllables looping together in a near continuous sound, his intonation rising and falling like a teeter-totter.

"From the moment we arrived, I knew something was different about this place. Something felt strange. Wrong. Like it wasn't alive."

"That's silly," said Lola, nudging him away protectively from their mother.

"I know how it sounds," he snapped, grabbing Lola's hand now as well, and holding both of them tightly, "but you have to believe me. I saw the book in the study—the ledger with all the names of the townspeople. Their birth dates, but no death records. That's because they've never died. And the portrait of that one girl on the wall—the same girl in the graveyard who did die, but a century and a half ago—it's Alice's sister."

"You're making this up," said Lola.

"Just listen. There's something you don't know. Last night I went back to the car and found Lola's external charger, and I saw them all—Doc Brown, Simon Sandborn, Lovicia—all the townspeople—and they were glowing in the moonlight like angels or aliens or something in between. And Alice told me how it happened. How they got sick with smallpox and then they encountered a strange creature and were somehow changed . . ."

Arlo explained everything to them—the one-paddled moose, the face in his window, Alice, the infected dress, the shadow grave, and the strange creature they called the Nameless.

"So, you see? We could stay here," he said finally, his eyes now clear and bright and hopeful. "You don't have to go to your appointment. We don't ever have to know if it's back or not. We could just stay right here in Livermore. Forever."

Arlo and his mother looked at each other long and hard, eyes unblinking like a staring contest. He was expecting her to tell him he was being ridiculous—that there was no such thing as magic or monsters, that the people in town were not a century and half old, that his fear, anxiety, and imagination had all spiraled out of control, creating this fantasy.

But if she didn't believe him, if she thought he had

lost all sense of reason and reality, she didn't reveal it. Instead she seemed thoughtful, contemplative, as though she was imagining the scenario as he described it.

"Arlo," she said at last, dredging herself up from where she'd been drifting. "I don't want you to worry . . . it's going to be okay."

There it was again. That worm in his brain. That awful, ugly worm. He dropped their hands.

"Stop saying that! Stop it!" The words exploded from him in a mixture of anger, frustration, and fear. Tears filled his eyes, and his body begin to tremble. "You don't know it will be okay! And saying it doesn't make it true!"

"Quit shouting," said Lola. She squared off with him, but their mother intervened.

"Arlo," she said calmly. "I know how hard this has been. All of it. And I've tried my best to protect you— both of you—from the sadness. But now I want you to listen to me. I can't promise you bad things won't ever happen. I can't tell you life will be perfect and as you hope and expect it to be. But I can tell you—promise you this—whatever happens, it will be okay. You will be okay."

He could see her thoughts churning. Before he could

say anything, she continued. "I've been thinking about that poem by Robert Frost and about what you said back in the car."

Arlo stood and scowled. Why was she talking about Robert Frost? Had she been listening to a word he'd said?

"You told me most people don't understand the poem—they get it wrong."

"Yes, but—"

"The thing is, I think everyone gets it wrong. There are two paths—and each is *equally fair*—and there are two meanings to the poem, each *equally fair*."

Arlo thought of the wrong turn they must have taken to end up in the mountains. Then he thought of the fork in the road—the path toward Livermore. He thought of the endless corridors in the mansion and the endless choices in life to turn left or turn right or to travel straight ahead.

"I think," continued his mother, "what Frost is really saying is you can take his poem to mean what you want it to mean, and you can choose whatever path you want to take. And in the end, it won't really matter because you'll have moved onward."

Though deep down, he knew she was right, Arlo wanted to stop her. To demand she focus. He blinked, and the tears he'd been fighting trickled down his cheeks. All his hopes and dreams were turning to ash in his heart. "But—" His voice cracked. "The Nameless . . . forever . . ."

She wiped his cheek tenderly. "If what you say is true—and I say if—then staying in Livermore is indecision. It's not moving forward. It's standing at the crossroads, never choosing, missing out on all the life ahead of you. Just like Mr. Kim said—you have to pick a path."

Arlo shook his head in a kind of silent misery. As much as he wanted to tell her she was wrong, he couldn't. Alice had said it was the living who held on to the dead. That the dead wanted to leave. Was that why she had mercilessly squashed the moth? Was it in fact merci*ful*?

"But we would be safe," he muttered. "And you wouldn't have to worry . . . I wouldn't have to worry . . ."

"I'm not worried," said his mother. "And besides." She gave him a playful jab. "I couldn't stay here. It's nice and all, but . . . there are no Larry's Licorice Laces in Livermore. You know how much I'd miss my favorite green candy."

Her face broke into a broad smile, crinkling her

cheeks and forcing lines into the corners of her eyes. She laughed, and her whole body shook with mirth so that Lola began to chuckle too. Even Arlo couldn't help but smile.

His mother wiped the laughter from her eyes and kissed Lola's forehead. The tension had just begun to leach out of the air when there came a sharp rap at the door.

"Dinner will be ready in an hour," said the crisp voice of Mrs. Hawthorn. "You're expected in the dining room."

Arlo's eyes shot to his mother. He didn't like the emphasis on the word *expected*. His expression seemed to plead with her to act inconspicuous. She understood and nodded, and then said cheerfully, "We'll be there. Thank you."

Alice's warning thudded in Arlo's ears. *There are those who would keep you and those who would get rid of you . . .* And suddenly he realized how foolish he'd been. How ridiculous. Stay in Livermore forever? What had he been thinking?

He swatted the remaining fog that had clouded his brain and took a deep breath, with pressed lips and flared nostrils. An intake of oxygen to bolster his courage. "If we're not going to stay, then we have to go," he said firmly. "We have to leave. Tonight. Before it's too late."

"Leave?" said Lola. "We can't leave. It'll be dark soon."

"We don't have a choice," he insisted. "We'll get to the car, pile on extra clothes, and wait for Dad. He's coming first thing in the morning. We should be there. Waiting."

"Mom?" whined Lola. "We can't leave now. This is Arlo we're talking about. Remember when he said we couldn't drink tap water anymore because it was dangerous? Or ride carnival rides? Or swim in lakes or the ocean? Or eat pickles?"

Arlo's mother looked at Lola. Then at Arlo. "I do recall us having to clear the house of thumbtacks."

His expression was fierce. "This is different. You have to believe me."

His mother studied his face for a moment. He could tell she didn't believe him but that she was trying very hard to. "Are you sure? Absolutely sure?"

"Yes," he said firmly. "We have to get out—while we still can."

"But," protested Lola, "I like it here."

Arlo's mother put her arm around her daughter. "It's not just Arlo. To tell you the truth, I've had a weird vibe ever since we came here, too. I just didn't want to say anything. Even if you don't believe Arlo, believe me. It's time. We should go."

It took some time to make a plan and convince Lola. After much protest and with great reluctance, she acquiesced and followed them into the hall. They had no belongings to carry, so there was nothing suspicious about their behavior.

Still, Mrs. Hawthorn patrolled the landing, *dusting*, she claimed. They exited and entered the room several times with some excuse or other. When at last, she was gone, they made their move.

Arlo kept a wary eye out lest they run into Woodbridge or Alice. If they did, he'd simply say they were going for a stroll.

The house was silent and still. They managed to make it to the foyer without running into a soul. They got their coats and shoes—or shoe, in his mother's case. Arlo glanced at the cracked cast. How would she survive the snow and the cold? He took off the extra wool socks he'd been wearing since the car and pulled them over his mother's cracked cast one at a time. It wasn't ideal, but it was better than nothing. They exited the mansion without being seen.

As the door clicked shut, Arlo was relieved to find

Hannah and the others were no longer sledding. The hill was empty, and the sun had dipped below the horizon and the sky was darkening by degrees and the moon was already visible, drifting in and out of passing clouds.

This was way too easy, he thought, eyeing the dark windows of the rickety houses they passed. He took his mother by the arm and propped her up as she limped along the path. Once they entered the woods, he'd find her a good branch she could use as a crutch.

Despite the cold, Arlo felt lighter. The oppressive mood weighing him down had lifted. Soon they would get to the car. His father wouldn't abandon them this time. He'd come as soon as he could—earlier if Arlo could manage to find a signal and text him to leave now. He'd pick them up, and his mother would receive the treatment for her ankle and make her appointment.

Arriving at the old bridge, Arlo stepped beneath the canopy of rickety timbers. What little light was left had dwindled such that the opening of the bridge was like a yawning mouth with a throat of darkness. The wood moaned and groaned as they entered, as though it was trying to swallow. He helped his mother through quickly, while Lola lagged behind, still unconvinced of this necessity and upset about having to leave Hannah without so much as a goodbye.

Arlo and his mother had exited the bridge and were making their way up the slope when he glanced back. Lola had stopped just outside the opening of the bridge. The darkening sky cast a purple shadow across her face. He was about to call to her, tell her to hurry, when the clouds parted and a ray of moonlight fell on her face and hands.

21

Arlo shut his eyes, but the image was still there, floating in the darkness of his mind. His head began to spin and the picture along with it—Lola, standing in the moonlight. Half her face glowed like cracked silver, one eye like a giant polished pearl. It was a monstrously hideous version of his little sister. The image turned faster and faster, getting smaller and smaller, until she disappeared into a pinpoint, a black hole inside his mind.

"Mom!" she cried. "Arlo!"

He opened his eyes, and it was like everything he knew—everything he thought he knew—had exploded into a billion pieces and fallen back into place but in an entirely different order. And in that moment, he finally understood.

This was what Alice had been trying to tell him. This was why the townsfolk could not decide what to do with them. Why they couldn't let them leave like the hikers and hunters who happened upon the town before them. They couldn't leave because Lola had been changed. Because Lola was one of them. The *one* they had spoken about.

His mother was by Arlo's side. Her mouth opened in slow motion, forming a perfect circle, and then froze. No words came out. Her face drained of color, and Arlo could tell from her pallor she was in shock.

They exchanged a single stricken look. His mother hadn't believed what he had tried to explain. Perhaps she had wanted to believe—like you want to believe in fairy tales and magic. Or perhaps she had felt so sorry for him that she believed *he* believed. But she herself hadn't. And how could she? It had all been too strange, too fantastical to imagine. Unless of course you'd seen it, witnessed it with your own eyes, like Arlo had. And now she had, too.

Lola was staring at the dazzling light emanating from her hand. She looked at it as though it didn't belong to her, as though it were at once something terrible and frightening and beautiful. Her expression was a blend of fear, incomprehension, and awe.

Arlo ran to her side and stopped short a foot away. Mist rose from her skin like dry ice evaporating through her pores. She looked cold, and Arlo resisted the urge to hug her to transfer his heat lest she burn him like the moose had burned his fingertips.

"H-How . . ." he breathed. "W-When . . ." His voice trailed off with puffs of his own breath into the cold dark night.

His mother was by his sister's side as well now. The color that had drained from her face returned in small increments. She reached out for Lola, babbling words of comfort, and in an instant, before she managed to touch her, it was over.

Black bloated clouds drifted over the moon, eclipsing its light, and just like that, Lola's hand and face appeared normal again. The shimmering glow and mist were gone as though they had been mere hallucinations.

Lola turned from her mother to Arlo, eyes wide, two perfect circles. It was as if she couldn't quite get the words out, as if she was imploring them silently, *What do I do?*

Arlo racked his brain. How had this happened? When had it happened? His thoughts bounced back to the first night they had arrived in Livermore. He remembered the spot on Lola's cheek that had glistened in the moonlight, the spot he had worried was the onset of frostbite. Lovicia had looked at Lola with a peculiar expression as well. She must have suspected it was there already, beneath her skin. Before they had even reached the town, Lola had already been infected.

Then he recalled something else. He reached out and gently turned her chin so that he had a good view of it. The circular scab on the side of her neck. The scab in the same spot as Alice's scar.

"I haven't felt cold," Lola whispered, as if talking to herself. "I haven't been hungry."

"Come on," said their mom, taking her daughter by the arm. "Let's get out of here."

Arlo didn't move. He understood now that sometimes what you wanted to do was not the same as what you had to do. He hung his head and murmured something so low it was barely audible. His mother must have heard him, though, as she stopped dead in her tracks and stared.

"What did you say?"

He closed his eyes and then opened them again. "I said, no. She can't go."

"What? What are you saying?"

"If she does," he said, "she'll stay like this forever. She won't get older. She won't change. People will turn her into a science experiment. They'll poke and prod or worse—she'll become some kind of sideshow exhibit. They won't leave her alone. Not ever. She won't have a life."

Arlo recalled the program he'd seen about the hiker who posted film footage to his social media of a Gigantopithecus—an extinct genus of ape. The post had gone viral, and soon the mountainside was swarming with people trying to capture the beast. Luckily, the footage turned out to be fake, but Arlo couldn't help but imagine what the mobs would have done to a poor creature if they'd caught it.

Arlo glanced at the dark silhouette of the town. Alice was right. People are cruel to those who are different, to people and things they don't understand. That was why the townsfolk stayed there. Isolated. Hidden. Safe.

"Then what do you suggest we do?" His mother's voice rose to squeaky territory. She stroked Lola's cheek and hair.

Arlo took a deep breath. "You have to go on. Alone."

"Don't be ridiculous," she said. "I'm not leaving you and Lola. I'd never leave you guys. Not in a million years."

"You have to," said Arlo. She began to protest again, but he stopped her. "Alice knew. She tried to tell me, but

I wouldn't listen. I have to go back. With Lola. I have to find Alice. She must know something we don't. Maybe she'll know what to do."

"No," insisted his mother, pulling Lola in close to her. "Not a chance. I can't leave you. I won't."

Lola's eyes glistened, but this time with tears. "Arlo's right. You have to go, Mom. He can fix this, can't you, Arlo?" She looked at him hopefully.

Arlo stared at her. He was terrified, and yet here she was trying so hard to be tough. He had to say something. He had to respond. How could he fix this? He had no idea if that was even possible. The one thing he was certain of was his mother needed to go. She couldn't run. Plus, she needed to get home for her ankle. And for her appointment.

"Yes," he lied. "I'm going to fix this. I'm going to fix everything, and we are going to get to the car. If you stay, it will be worse for us. You'll only hold us back. If we have to make a run for it, you'll be too slow."

He made excellent arguments, but he could tell his mother wasn't having any of it. How could he get her to understand? What could he say? And then it came to him. That simple phrase. He took her hand and squeezed.

"It's going to be okay."

Arlo's mother paused. She looked at him with a phantom smile. He'd struck a chord. She was smart. She was logical. She knew she was in bad shape. To leave them was to help them. It was the only way. She knew they were right, but Arlo could tell she was fighting it.

"Dad is coming," he said reassuringly. "He promised, and I have to believe in him one more time. Here. Take my phone." He handed it to her. "Get to the car, then try for a signal. If you reach him, tell him to leave now, this very second. He'll listen to you."

She took the phone and began to argue one last time.

"We have to go back now. Before they know we're missing. I need to get to Alice. There's not much time. We'll meet you at the car as soon as we can. If we're not there by morning . . ."

"You will be," she said resolutely. Arlo nodded.

There were so many emotions on her face it was impossible to untangle them. But one stood out—one he had never seen there before—but one he recognized immediately. Fear. Large tears tumbled down her cheeks as she nodded, wrapped her arms around both of them, and squeezed as hard as she could, then broke the embrace.

Arlo and Lola walked her up the hill. They helped her over the low wall and stood facing each other.

"Find the car and wait for us there," said Arlo.

His mother raised her chin and swiped at her cheeks. "I'll be there." She took a deep breath, nodded, and then turned and hobbled along the path. She waved to them once and then was swallowed up by the dark woods.

Arlo took one last look at the spot where his mother had disappeared and felt a painful tug. He looked at Lola and smiled weakly. "Come on." He took her by the hand. It was ice-cold, but it didn't burn. He turned his face toward the town, and together, they descended the path and entered the old bridge.

Arlo recalled that first morning they had arrived in Livermore. Only three short days earlier, it felt like a lifetime ago. He recalled the unsettling feeling he'd had back then, staring at the dark, abandoned-looking structures, and yet here he was, returning once again.

As he walked, he scanned the darkness. Without the moonlight, it was black as pitch. Still, there was something, a certain quality to the air, a thickening of shadows that caused the empty space around him to thrum. And suddenly, he had an unmistakable feeling, a strange tickling of the senses, like someone was out there. Watching him.

He and Lola were approaching Lovicia's house when

the feeling overpowered him. The clouds were thinning. They still shrouded the moon, but enough light bounced off the snow, illuminating the air. They froze. There, on the road, not ten feet from them, stood Alice, the dark silhouette of her body thin and angular, like a baby bird that had left its nest prematurely.

For a moment no one spoke. She looked at Lola, then at Arlo, and he saw it in her expression. She knew. And Arlo couldn't tell if the look in her eye was one of gloom or triumph. He opened his mouth to ask her for help, but before he could, someone spoke.

"Well, well. What do we have here?"

Arlo turned to face the old cottage. Though he was in front of her house, Lovicia's sudden appearance wrong-footed him.

She gazed up at the sky like the witch in *The Wizard of Oz* fearing a flying house might drop on her. With the moon still partially hidden behind the clouds, she stepped out of the door, onto the porch, and stood hands on her hips, as tall and imposing as a stone statue.

"Leaving at last?"

Arlo was no actor. In second grade, his class had performed *The Little White Rabbit Who Wanted Red Wings*. All the other students had been rabbits and ducks and squirrels, but he had been cast as a slug. His teacher, Ms.

Spitz, had told him to just crouch on the stage and remain still for the duration of the play.

"You're a natural," she'd praised him after the show, but he had no illusions. He couldn't even throw himself down on the soccer field and feign injury like the other boys on his team. How would he be able to act as though nothing was wrong?

He swallowed hard and forced a shaky smile—a mask of cheerfulness obscuring a chasm of fear. "We . . . we were . . . we were just . . ."

"They were with me," said Alice, turning her attention toward Lovicia. The two eyed each other, and once again Arlo had the distinct feeling a message was passing between them. When Alice continued, it was odd. Arlo couldn't tell if she was explaining or instructing.

"I've been watching them, as everyone knows," said Alice. Lovicia nodded curtly. "They wanted to go for a walk, and the night is dark. There's no moonlight. I thought they might get lost."

Lovicia pursed her thin lips and nodded again. Arlo couldn't tell what exactly was happening. And then, as if matters could possibly get worse, more shadows appeared just beyond Alice. It was Hannah, Woodbridge, Martha Lovering, and Simon Sandborn.

"What's going on?" asked Woodbridge.

"You should be inside," said Simon.

"It's dangerous out here," said Martha with a sickly sweet lilt.

Alice turned from Lovicia to face the others. "They were with me," she repeated. "They wanted a walk. There's no moonlight. I thought they'd get lost."

Woodbridge nodded and smiled, seemingly believing his daughter. But Hannah's eyes narrowed. She was smiling, too, but for the first time, Arlo had a sense of what lay behind her mask.

"Where is your mother?" She spoke softly, but she sounded less like a little girl and more like an ancient queen or wicked sorceress. Imposing. Imperious.

Arlo's heart plummeted. He cast his eyes downward. This was it. They were caught. Even Alice couldn't explain their way out this time. All was lost. He moved closer to Lola and then . . .

"She's resting," said a voice. And even though Arlo had looked up in time to see her say it, a shock of surprise rocked his whole body.

"She didn't feel well as they passed my cottage," said Lovicia, "so I told her to come in and rest awhile in my bed."

Martha Lovering eyed Lovicia. "She's inside? In your bed?"

A curiously intense expression came into Lovicia's eyes. "Yes. Now, best you all go back and have dinner. I'll make sure she's okay." She flicked a hand at them dismissively.

Martha stood motionless. Woodbridge looked at Alice and nodded, and even Hannah, whose gaze lingered a little longer on Lovicia, accepted the explanation.

"Yes," said Hannah, at last. "Let's all go back. Dinner will get cold." She smiled, took Lola by the hand, and led her toward the mansion.

Lola glanced over her shoulder at Arlo. He forced a reassuring smile. Then he turned briefly toward Lovicia. His head dipped once, almost imperceptibly, as if to say thank you. She frowned and shut her door.

Leave. While you still can . . .

Her words echoed in Arlo's mind as he followed Alice and the others back up the hill. He had thought they had been a threat, but he'd had it all wrong. It had been a warning.

Arlo caught up to Alice, who lagged behind, waiting for him. He leaned in close. "Is there a way?" he whispered. "Can she change back?"

Alice was quiet. She watched the others, making sure they were a safe distance ahead. "Yes," she said softly.

22

"There is a way . . ." Alice began in a wistful, somewhat stilted manner. She stood by the fireplace in Arlo's bedroom, staring at the glowing embers as if longing to feel even a hint of warmth.

Arlo hung alongside her, rubbing his hands. He'd barely eaten a bite during dinner, which took forever. When he'd explained he felt a chill and thought he might be coming down with a cold, Woodbridge Samuels and Martha Lovering had chuckled unexpectedly, as though he'd made some sort of joke.

Lola sat quietly on the edge of the bed. Alice turned from the fire to face Arlo, her eyes hooded, her expression solemn. "She must become unchanged."

In spite of the heat, Arlo felt suddenly stone-cold.

He looked at Lola, her face swollen with concern. *Unchanged* had an awful implication. It implied a reversal of the process. And there was only one thing that could achieve that. The Nameless.

There was a silence in which Arlo absorbed this new information. The risk. The danger. Nevertheless, it all crystallized into the only possible course of action.

"There has to be another way," he muttered. But it came out weak, like he was trying to come to terms with what he knew to be true and yet couldn't bear to accept.

Alice took the metal tongs and prodded the logs. "If Lola is not unchanged, she will remain like us. The years will accumulate around her like so much dust on a windowpane, and then before you know it, it will be too late." She flicked Arlo a glance that suggested: *If it isn't already.*

"What do you mean?" he said. But Alice stared emptily at the orange embers stirred to life.

"Arlo?" said Lola.

He swallowed his fear. "Don't worry. I won't leave you here."

"She can't leave either," said Alice. "If you take her away, you'll see just how cruel the world can be. Better to face the Nameless than an angry mob calling you wretched monster, evil witch, threatening to drown you or burn you."

He shuddered. What had these people endured? He glanced at his sister. Times had changed, but the cruelty of humans hadn't. If anyone had an inkling of Lola's condition, who knew what sort of experiments they'd do? It was clear to him—Lola could neither leave nor stay in Livermore. *Unchanged* was the only alternative.

"But what is it?" he asked.

Alice shook her head. "There are many mysteries in this world. This is one of them."

"But . . . is it d-dangerous?" asked Lola.

"It hasn't harmed me," she said.

Lola looked at Arlo for reassurance.

He was more than exhausted—he was shattered—but he inhaled and forced a smile. "It'll be okay, Lo."

Alice cast him a third, grave look. She leaned in close and whispered, "She's been changed for a reason. Something was wrong. The Nameless can't fix you. It halts a process. If she is unchanged, she'll return to the state she was in. Not dead—but probably close to it."

"How do you know?" asked Arlo. "Has anyone ever been unchanged?"

She cast her gaze downward, and Arlo detected such deep sorrow in her tone. "Once."

Arlo didn't like the sound of this. He moved toward the bed and took his sister by the hands. "Listen. I know when this happened. I just don't know why. We need to figure out why."

Lola nodded vigorously.

"Think back. We were in the car. Mom and I were talking. You were playing your game . . ."

"I was playing Cruise Crunch . . ."

"Yes. Right. And then what?"

She closed her eyes. Her eyebrows furled. She was thinking hard. Very hard.

"We had the accident," said Arlo. "I found you outside the car. You were sitting with your back against the tree. What happened to you, Lo? How did you get there?"

"I'm not sure," she said tentatively. She opened her eyes. A watery skin was forming over them. "I was playing the game. I was eating the apple. Then it all happened so fast. I flew forward and then snapped back when the seat belt pulled tight. We were spinning and spinning. And then we hit again—this time harder. And then . . .

Arlo stood. "And then what?"

"And then I was calling for you. For Mom. But I had no voice. I couldn't breathe. Something was wrong. Really wrong. I got out of the car. I was trying to breathe, but I couldn't. I was so scared, Arlo. I wanted to scream, but I couldn't make a sound. I was falling.

I sunk down against the tree. The world was slipping away. I couldn't hold on."

"Then what? Come on. Keep going," he urged.

"I don't remember anything else. Not until my body began to burn. I was on fire. Like I was being boiled. And then all of a sudden, the burning stopped and I was cold. So cold. I thought for sure I was dead. But then . . ."

"Then you saw it? You saw the Nameless?"

She shook her head. "Then I heard you calling my name, and I opened my eyes. I started coughing. I threw up and then . . ."

Arlo turned and began pacing. He racked his brain. She'd been playing the game. She'd been eating her apple. The car hit the tree . . .

He thought back to his first aid course. She had no external injuries. No bruises. No blood. It was possible she had internal injuries, but she hadn't been thrown from the car—she'd exited it on her own. That was good. He ran his fingers through his hair, scratching his scalp to invigorate his brain cells.

She'd been playing the game. She'd been eating. She couldn't breathe or make a sound, and then . . . and then . . .

All at once, as though a great boulder had landed

smack-dab on top of him, squashing him, it was clear. He practically couldn't breathe himself, but in that instant, he knew. He knew what had happened to Lola—he was nearly certain—and if he was right—he knew he could fix it.

"We need to go," he said firmly. "We need to find the Nameless. Now."

"No one has seen it in nearly a century," said Alice.

"But why us? Why Lola?"

Alice shrugged. "You must have woken it when you hit the old tree. The roots grow deep underground. They tangle, intertwining with one another like a great tapestry. Pull one thread, you pull them all." She smiled faintly. "But I know where to find it. I know a way into the burrow."

Lola gulped "Burrow?"

"Perfect. So, what are we waiting for?" said Arlo. "Let's go."

"Not yet. My father, Mrs. Hawthorn, and Martha will be in the parlor discussing tonight's meeting. The whole town will be gathering at midnight to settle your fate. Once and for all."

"We'll sneak out the front door," he said.

She shook her head. "Doc Brown and Simon Sandborn are watching outside. They suspect you know something. Especially since your unexpected stroll. Everyone is worried you might try to escape."

"Then what do we do?"

"Wait here," she continued. "When all leave for the meeting, I'll go with them. It will be dark. I'll slip away and come back for you. We'll have to be quick, though. Once they arrive at the meeting place, they'll know I'm not there. They'll come for us—for you—and then it will be too late."

A fluttering panic rose up inside him. Was Alice telling the truth? Or would she betray them? He couldn't tell.

"But what if Hannah discovers my mother isn't in Lovicia's bed? What if Lovicia tells her? They'll come for us."

"She won't."

"How do you know? How can you be so sure?"

"I trust Lovicia. We've been friends for a very, very long time . . ."

Lola's face pinched. "You're friends with Hannah's aunt?"

"Hannah's aunt?" Alice said, slightly taken aback. "Is that what they told you?"

Arlo looked at Lola, then back at Alice. "Isn't she?"

"She's not Hannah's aunt." Alice smiled, unable to hide her amusement. "She's her little sister."

Once again, the world around Arlo began to spin. He felt like he was on a carnival ride.

"But . . . but how is that even possible?" asked Lola.

"Lovicia didn't get ill with the pox. She grew up and got old and became ill much later. She had a weak heart. Doc said she wouldn't live long. But I knew where to find the Nameless. I took her one night to get changed. We never told the others how she came across it. It's been our secret."

Arlo didn't know what to believe anymore. Hannah, the eight-year-old, was older than the old woman, Lovicia. And Alice. Alice was over a hundred. It was all too much for him. He suddenly felt wobbly. "So, what do we do?"

"Stay here. Wait. Do not leave this room," she said firmly. "I'll return. I promise." The door creaked open, and she slipped out into the hallway. Arlo listened as her footsteps descended the stairs.

"What did Alice mean? What's wrong with me?" whispered Lola.

Arlo took a deep breath. Should he tell her what he knew—what he thought he knew? If he did, she might panic. He couldn't have her panic. Not now. It would make things so much worse. "Do you trust me?" he asked.

Lola held his gaze. His eyes remained steady, unblinking. It seemed to reassure her. She nodded. "Of course."

"Then leave it to me. I won't let you down."

She nodded, turned away from him, and lay down on the bed. He watched her intently as she inhaled, her ribs expanding and contracting beneath her clothing. It told Arlo something very important.

They sat quietly for some time, and then Lola asked, "Do you think Mom made it to the car?"

Arlo had been wondering the same thing. It was possible, but unlikely given her speed. "Soon," he reassured Lola. "And she'll be fine once she gets there."

Arlo stood and stared out the window into the darkness of the night. Without his phone, he felt lost. How much time had passed? One hour? Two? Three? All the while, Lola lay on her side. She closed her eyes, and he wasn't sure if she'd drifted off.

Arlo left the window and sat in a chair by the woodstove. The last embers were getting cold. Where was Alice? What was taking her so long? He tried to remain calm, but with each minute that passed, more doubt crept into his heart. At last he could wait no longer. He got up and moved toward the door. He reached for the knob, but it turned on its own. The door creaked open, and Alice reentered carrying an oil lantern.

"Where have you been? What took you so long?" He was certain it must be approaching midnight.

"There's no time to explain." She moved toward Lola and jiggled her gently. "We need to move. Quickly."

"It's time," said Arlo, pulling Lola to her feet. "Let's go."

"Ready," said Lola, yawning and rubbing her eyes.

They stepped quickly and quietly into the hallway, down the enormous staircase, and into the front hall, the glow of the lantern lighting their way. They found their shoes, grabbed their jackets, and fled the mansion without looking back. Arlo couldn't escape the feeling it was all too easy.

The night was cold, the ground hard, and the dusting of snow made it slippery. He nearly lost his footing as they raced down the hill toward the houses, past Lovica's and the other dark houses, and on to the covered bridge.

"Quickly," Alice said as she ducked beneath the canopy of rotting timber. "We have a long way to go."

The clouds hid the moon, but Arlo had a sudden flashback of his sister's face, silvery webs running beneath her skin, one eye an enormous glowing pearl.

He shook the image loose and reached for her hand. He pulled Lola into the tunnel, along the rickety planks, and out the other side.

Alice was far ahead. She seemed to know exactly where to place her feet in the darkness, avoiding dips and holes, diverging from the path and disappearing into the woods. Arlo hurried to catch up, following the lantern's glow like a lost ship toward a lighthouse.

The wind had picked up. It howled through the bare branches. It was as though the old forest had come alive once again, warning him, taunting him. As Arlo followed Alice further into the dark, malevolent place, thin tendrils of icy mist rose from the ground, whirling about their feet like vaporous snakes, climbing trunks and coiling about blackened limbs.

They had been running at least a half hour when at last, Alice came to a halt in front of an enormous oak. On the side of its massive trunk, between mad patterns of thick, tangled roots, she pointed to a spot where the earth had given way. A black hole the size of a sewer grate opened up. The darkness pulled and sucked at him.

"Here," she said.

Arlo looked at Lola. He didn't need light to know her face had lost all color.

"I-In there?" she said with a trembling voice.

"Yes," said Alice. Without another word, she placed the lantern on the ground, got to her knees, maneuvered her body, and dropped feet first into the darkness below. Only the tips of her fingers breached the surface. "The light."

Arlo lowered the lantern into her waiting hands. He steeled himself. "I'll go next."

As he lowered himself into the pit, the echo of the river, the hooting of owls, all the forest sounds faded into cool silence. Smells he couldn't begin to identify assaulted him. Pungent, dank, and sour.

He had had no idea what to expect, had braced himself, and yet was surprised nonetheless to find himself in a narrow space large enough to stand without crouching. The ground beneath his feet was spongy, and water dripped down from somewhere above, beating a steady rhythm on a hard surface—perhaps a rock or stone.

"Your turn, Lo," he called, reaching a hand up to her. She took it, and he caught her as she came down.

In the lantern glow, he surveyed the subterranean landscape. They were in a hollow that moved onward, tunneling in several directions. The ceiling was crowned with intertwining roots—the tapestry Alice had described. The walls were earth and rock, mined by something very sharp. Dead leaves, rotting vegetation, and who knew what else littered the ground, congealing into a black slime. He wondered how long it would be before spiders would drop down onto him, crawling on his skin and through his hair.

"This way," said Alice, holding the lantern in front of her, taking the tunnel to Arlo's right. She walked a few feet and then stopped, marking a large X in the ground with the tip of her shoe.

"What's that for?" asked Arlo.

"The web is complex. It's long and winding. This will help you find your way out," she said, adding quickly, "if we are separated."

Arlo didn't like this place, nor the use of the word *web* to describe it. It was dark and claustrophobic. He looked back over his shoulder. The opening to the ground above was already lost beyond the reach of the lantern's dim glow. He shuddered at the thought of becoming lost in the underground labyrinth.

"Stay close," he said, taking Lola by the hand.

They followed Alice for some time, taking one tunnel then another, turning this way and that, heading downward and then upward. Every ten to twenty feet, she marked the ground with another X. Arlo was careful to step over the markings, leaving them intact. The air was thin, and it was getting harder to breathe.

"Almost there," said Alice, after what felt like forever.

Arlo had lost all sense of time and place. He had no idea how far or how deep they'd gone. When Alice came to a halt so suddenly, Arlo nearly bumped into her. Ahead, the narrow tunnel ballooned into a large chamber, which the weak lamplight failed to fully penetrate.

The fine hair on the back of Arlo's neck sent him an alarm. He felt a presence, though his eyes could not as yet see any. A rank odor filled his nostrils as his heart thudded a warning. Had Alice betrayed them? Were the townspeople there waiting?

"Stand very still," whispered Alice. Arlo and Lola halted while she inched further into the earthy abyss.

At first, Arlo saw nothing but the empty chamber walls of mud and stone. But then Alice reached up and gently tugged on a root. His senses sharpened as he caught movement overhead.

Slowly, a shadow disentangled itself from the root ceiling. It crept downward, into the light. Panic rendered Arlo's breath shallow and weak, and his grip tightened on his sister's hand.

The figure that emerged from the roots unfolded itself in a strange and silent choreography until it was large and looming. Though grotesquely distorted, it had a vaguely human outline, with rudimentary limbs, spindly, insect-like, and connecting to the body in knots of gris-tle. Each ended in talons, perfect for mining the earth and stone. It had an aura of antiquity—as though it had lived for eons.

The head was pulpy and misshapen, a fusion of faces. The creature was earthy in tone, faintly greenish in the lantern light, but the eyes glistened bluish silver like the metallic blue shells of milkweed beetles. They rolled in sockets before settling on the three children.

Nothing Arlo had ever seen in real life or fantasy came remotely close to the hideous and frightful sight. Even the creatures in *Zombie Army of Darkness* seemed tame in comparison.

What had Alice done by bringing them here? A sat-isfied grin stole across her thin lips, and there was an almost predatory slant to her eyes as the beast rose to its full height and let loose a guttural cry.

Lola screamed, and Arlo tucked her instinctively behind his back. He held his arm, elbow bent, over his face to shield them from any blows.

"It's okay," whispered Alice, and Arlo wasn't sure if she was talking to him or the beast.

When no assault came, Arlo slowly lowered his arm to discover the large body had stooped, its head now inches from his face. There was a brief moment in which he attempted to relearn the skill of breathing, while the thing appeared to study him, sense him, get a feel for who and what he was. Arlo did the same, taking in the silvery cold stare of the metallic eyes.

"If you're sure," said Alice, "then bring out Lola."

"B-But . . . how . . . ?" His voice was so small and

unrecognizable, as though any sound from his lips might trigger an onslaught.

"Go on," she said. "There's not much time. They'll be looking for us already."

While the ghoulish head remained close to his, its fetid odor filling his mind and body, he thought back to the accident. To Lola. To what he believed had happened to her.

"I'm ready," he said, stepping aside. He could feel his sister's averseness, her trembling hands, so he added, "Don't worry. I've got you, Lo."

"Unchange," said Alice. She tilted her head, swept her hair aside, and pointed to her scar.

At first, the monster gave no indication it heard or understood. Then, suddenly it leaned in close, examining Lola.

"Arlo?" said Lola, turning her head away, revealing her own scar in the process.

"I will fix this," he said, hoping it was the truth. "Promise."

Before she could respond, there came a sudden shocking movement. What looked like a telescope propelled from one of the creature's many faces. It hit Lola with the speed of a lizard's tongue snatching a fly. It connected with the scab on her neck near her artery.

Lola screamed. Arlo moved instinctively to protect her, but Alice gripped his arm and held him back.

"Let it be," she said.

He watched in horror as Lola's face and neck glowed silver for a moment, the substance beneath it retreating back into the creature like a reverse snakebite. Like a reverse vampire.

It was over so quickly, Arlo didn't have time to think, let alone speak. The creature retreated, and Arlo watched Lola, her eyes turned slowly toward him, her mouth hanging open in the scream that had now fallen silent.

With the silver pattern gone, her face turned blue. Her eyes closed, and she dropped to the ground with a soft thud. Arlo fell to her side. As he suspected, she wasn't breathing.

Before the accident, Lola had been eating the apple. When they hit the tree, Arlo was sure a piece had become lodged in her throat. She couldn't breathe. She couldn't speak because she had been choking. He knew from his first aid course that full obstruction was not loud but dangerously silent.

Arlo had been preparing for this moment. He knew CPR. He only hoped it wasn't too late.

Positive thoughts, he told himself. Positive thoughts. And without a moment's hesitation, he began . . .

Step one. Area check. It was true they were in an underground cave, but nonetheless he did a quick sweep. No fire. No wire. No gas. No glass.

Next, he dropped to his knees beside his sister, pinched her ear, and yelled, "Hey, Hey, Hey—are you okay?" to be sure he hadn't missed something and she wasn't conscious. You must never perform CPR on someone who is conscious.

Since 911 wasn't an option, he skipped to the next step. He rolled her over so that she was on her back, facing upward. He did a head tilt–chin lift and checked her ABCs—airways, breathing, and circulation—to make sure she wasn't breathing.

She hadn't been in water, so he began with thirty compressions. He interlocked his fingers, straightened his elbows, and locked them. He found the proper spot in the center of her rib cage and pumped to the beat of the old song, "Staying Alive."

After completing thirty compressions, he did another head tilt–chin lift to open her airways and then gave her two breaths. Her chest rose, then fell. He checked. She still wasn't breathing.

His own heart was beating a mile a minute. "Come on, Lola!" he yelled. "Breathe!"

Thoughts of Alice and the creature were driven from his mind. They had faded into the background as he focused on Lola and began the cycle again. Thirty compressions. Twenty-seven. Twenty-eight. Twenty-nine . . . And two breaths.

"Breathe!" he begged. "Breathe, Lo!"

Still nothing. Panic rose in Arlo's throat. It threatened to choke him. He had promised his sister he would fix this. He'd told her he would. She'd believed him. She was counting on him. He couldn't let her down.

Arlo began a third cycle. Then a fourth. Tears were streaming down his cheeks. His arms ached. But he wouldn't give up. Positive thoughts. Positive thoughts.

He began a fifth cycle. Ten compressions . . . fifteen . . . And then at long last, Lola's eyelids fluttered. He stopped the compressions and watched as her chest rose and fell ever so slightly on its own.

"Yes!" he screamed. "Yes!" Alice raced to his side and gave him a hug.

Lola opened her eyes. There was bewilderment in her expression. She blinked and sat up. She looked around at the chamber, at Arlo and Alice, then at the creature.

"Where am I? What is tha—that thing?" she asked. She was pale and confused, obviously in shock. Arlo flung his arm around her and squeezed.

"Not . . . so . . . tight," she muttered.

Arlo and Alice grinned. Lola was weak, very weak, but there was no time to treat her for shock. He pulled her to her feet and propped her upright. He looked at the strange creature, which seemed more magical than threatening, and then turned to Alice.

"Let's go."

"Follow the X's," she said. "You'll find your way out."

Arlo stared at her a moment, trying to make sense of her words. "But . . . what about you?"

"You're not far from the road. You'll find it. Go quickly. They'll be searching for you."

"But . . . aren't you coming?" he asked.

"My mother hadn't been happy," she said. "She missed her dear Libby. She didn't enjoy living—if you can call it that—in this condition."

The creature moved toward her.

"She followed me when I brought Lovicia here. She warned Lovicia this wasn't a natural existence. It wasn't how things were meant to be. But I convinced Lovicia to join us."

Alice's voice broke off. She took a deep breath. "Mother had had enough. She said this was a fate she wouldn't wish on an enemy. She wanted to become unchanged. And she was. Just like Lola. Just like I will be."

The reality of what was happening—what Alice was about to do—came tumbling down on Arlo like an avalanche of dread. He couldn't let her do it.

"No!" he said.

"You mustn't worry," she said. "I don't fear death. That pang has long passed."

"Don't!" He lunged for her.

"Stay back!"

The force of her fury beat against him like icy waves, driving him backward. In the same instant, the creature sent its telescoped mouth to her neck and sucked back the silvery substance that had kept her alive over a hundred years.

There was a moment when Alice hung somewhere between life and death, not part of one world or the other. She looked at Arlo, and as their eyes met, she smiled— and it was warm and happy. And free.

How could he have mistrusted her? How could he have ever believed she would harm him? He wanted to reach out, to grasp her, to hold on to her, to keep her here, in this world. But then he remembered her words. They echoed in the caverns of his mind. *The living try to hold on, but . . . The dead want to leave.*

She stood there a moment, frozen in space and time. And then there was a shudder, a soft sigh, and all the lost years began to ripple through her body, slowly at first, then picking up speed.

Her flesh grew red and hot. Her skin bubbled with smallpox blisters. And then it stopped and shrunk, turning wooden at first, and then ashen and dead. Her soft hair became dry and dusty. Her eyes sunk deeper and deeper, until they were nothing but great black chasms. The flesh that clung to her bones bit by bit disintegrated until she was gone, winked out of existence, her dust scattering to the ground, like she had never been.

The beast let loose another earsplitting cry, and though Arlo was sure it was a cry filled with sorrow and lament, without Alice, he was suddenly frightened again. Alice was gone. There was no bringing her back. And there was no time to wonder about the person she had once been. No time to grieve her passing. No time to say thank you. Or goodbye.

The world that had briefly stopped began turning again, and Arlo found his feet. He placed his arm under

Lola's shoulder, propping her up, and took the lantern in the other. Together they raced as quickly as Lola could manage out of the chamber into the labyrinth of tunnels, darting this way and that, following the X's Alice had so cleverly placed until they found the gaping hole in the earth.

Arlo heard a final cry, muted and obscure, and then dropped the lantern and hoisted a breathless Lola until she was out in the open. He passed her the lantern and then sprang up, snatching a root above the ground, and with Lola's help, he pulled himself out of the hole.

He lay on the cold, hard ground breathing in the fresh air, happy to be out of the underground maze, but before he could catch his breath, he heard a voice in the distance.

"There they are!" shouted Hannah. "Over there!"

Arlo clambered to his feet. He snatched up the oil lantern and hurled it as far as he could. It crashed against a large tree trunk, where it exploded into a ball of fire. He grasped Lola's hand, and supporting her as best he could, they raced away from the flames.

The clouds had cleared. Trails of mist and twisted moonbeams filled the dark forest. Trees loomed like skeletal shadows, dangling bony-limbed branches. He darted and dodged, checking over his shoulder as he ran. Glistening faces dappled the landscape converging on the burning lamp.

Arlo had no idea where he was, nor how far it was to the path or to the main road. He had been so focused on following Alice that he had lost any and all sense of direction. How would he ever find his way to the car?

"I see movement!" shouted Simon Sandborn.

"Over there!" said Martha Lovering.

Silver faces wove through the mist and moonlight, and for a moment Arlo could have sworn he was in an episode of *Zombie Army of Darkness*. What would Dr. Zoid do? *Don't panic*, he heard Zoid tell him. *Positive thoughts . . . Positive thoughts . . .* said Dr. Lewis.

Lola was weary. It took all his strength to hold her upright and drag her along with him. His chest pounded, and his legs grew heavy, as though they were tethered to the surrounding tree trunks.

"Get them!" said Hannah.

"Don't let them escape," said Doc Brown.

"Alice!" yelled Woodbridge. "Does anyone see Alice?"

Thoughts howled in Arlo's brain. His insides gave a twist. The image of Alice fading to nothingness swam in the darkness before his eyes. Was it his fault? Was it because of him that she had decided it was time to go? Now, more than ever, he wanted to race from this sad and ugly fairy tale.

The townsfolk were getting closer. Arlo's bones hummed, and his muscles strained. His legs cramped. His stomach cramped. His quadriceps ignited in pain. Lactic acid burned in his spent muscles making his stomach churn. His lungs were going to collapse.

Lola was slowing. He didn't know how much longer he'd be able to run with her in tow, and for all he knew, he was going in circles. At last, she slipped from his grasp and dropped to the ground.

"Get up," he whispered.

"I—I can't."

He wrenched Lola to her feet. "I'll distract them." His voice was so quiet, he barely heard it himself. "You have to run." He nudged her, but she held tight. "Come on, Lola," he begged. There would only be one chance.

She shook her head and then went limp in his arms. "You go. Leave me."

Panic rushed into his mind like a swarm of angry hornets. Arlo's thoughts scrambled. He wouldn't leave his sister. But they couldn't run either—not now—she needed rest. There was another way, he thought suddenly. Another chance.

They had to hide.

Pulling Lola, Arlo ducked behind a large tree trunk with a deep hollow between its thick roots. He urged Lola downward, forcing her into the tight space, and then crouched beside her. He cupped his hand gently over her mouth to keep her quiet. They'd have to stay silent and still and hope not to be seen.

The darkness provided a thin shield. The smell of

damp earth and decomposition enveloped him. He held his breath, pressed his face into Lola's arm and waited. He counted out the beats of his own heart until he felt them slow to a less frenzied pace, but his brain was awash with dizzying thoughts.

He recalled the day his mother brought Lola home from the hospital. His father told him he was getting a huge surprise. He had imagined a new football. An enormous ice cream cake. A puppy. A trip to the moon. He was more than disappointed when they presented him with the chubby sleeping baby. And though he told them he'd have much preferred the football, he had also agreed to always take care of her.

Seconds turned to minutes and minutes passed like hours. Glowing bodies flitted like fireflies between the trees, voices calling in the dark. After what felt like ten lifetimes, the voices began to fade. When, at last, Arlo lifted his head and risked a peek, the glowing bodies had drifted like distant ghostly mist, and Arlo knew this was their chance.

They had to be quick. He helped Lola out of the hollow and to her feet. Though she had regained a little of her strength, he still needed to prop her up. The forest was thick and dark and he had no idea which way to go. He turned in a slow circle.

"Is she gone?" said a voice.

It came from behind him, making him jump. His heart plummeted. He was sweating. Shaking. They had been caught. He released Lola and swung round, eyes wide in the darkness.

Then, the figure removed the kerchief that was wrapped about her head. The skin was incandescent, but the face was familiar. "Is she gone? Is Alice gone?"

There was no malice in Lovicia's voice, just a kind of sad curiosity.

Arlo stepped forward into the moonlight and nodded once. "Yes."

"Was it . . . painful?" Lovicia placed her fingertips lightly on the circular scar on the side of her neck.

"I don't think so. I think . . ." he said, his voice catching in his throat, "I think she was . . . relieved."

Lovicia's eyes were large and iridescent, like polished white opals. There was a magic in them that was both remarkable and frightening. She looked down at her own hands, glistening like cracked silver, and Arlo knew she was contemplating Alice's decision.

Was she, too, tired of her never-ending existence? Would she, too, find the courage and go like Alice one day? One thing was certain—both Alice and Lovicia had wanted to protect them from what they believed to be a fate worse than death.

Lovicia wrapped the kerchief around her head again and tucked her hands into her coat pockets. "Follow me," she said, turning her back on them. "I'll take you to the road, but be quick."

They moved quickly, trunk to trunk, shadow to shadow, following Lovicia. Arlo couldn't see any of the other townsfolk, but there would be no relief until he was safely out of the woods and far away from Livermore.

It took some time, but at last they arrived on the path not far from the crossroads. He could see the old wooden sign in the distance. They weren't far from the main road and the car now.

"Find your mother. Take her and go," said Lovicia. "Never return to Livermore. Never."

Arlo took one last look at her milky eyes. It was hard to imagine this old woman as a young girl—younger than Alice. Younger than Hannah.

"Thank you," he said. "For everything."

"Yes," said Lola.

Lovicia did not respond. She simply turned and retreated into the folds of darkness. She was gone.

"Almost there," said Arlo. Lola was leaning heavily

on him, but the crossroads were close. Another hundred feet or so, and they'd be on the main road. His heart began to swell. They had made it. Together they hobbled as fast as they could, like the winning team in a three-legged race.

"Leaving so soon?" A figure stepped out of the darkness, into a patch of moonlight directly ahead of them.

Lola froze and Arlo along with her. "H-Hannah," she stammered.

Arlo's throat went dry, and he croaked as he fumbled for an excuse. "We were—we were just looking for—for Alice, and . . ." He tried to say the words lightly, but they felt strange and heavy in his mouth.

Hannah's face and hands were translucent. The veins beneath them glowed silverfish blue like the beetle-back eyes of the Nameless. But whereas Lovicia had seemed somehow wondrous, Hannah was ghoulish. Like a little, evil, bewitched china doll.

She shook her head. "The time for lies has passed, don't you think?" Her voice was calm. Casual, even.

Time slowed as they stood staring at each other. Arlo forced his breathing to slow to quiet the tremor in his voice. He gripped his hands into tight fists, wracking his brain for an appeal that might persuade her.

"We won't tell anyone," he said firmly. "Not about you. Or the town. Leave us alone. And we'll leave you alone."

"Ah. But that's just it," said Hannah, with a calm, almost detachment. "I am alone. And lonely. Very lonely."

"I don't understand," squeaked Lola. "What do you want from us?"

Hannah was a menacing blur of bluish-white light. Arlo's teeth began to chatter. He clamped his jaw to stop it from moving. He willed Lola to remain alert for the chance to run. He sent her a silent message—*please run, Lola, please*—but she didn't move.

"It was nice having someone new around," said Hannah. "A new friend. New blood . . ."

"You're not my friend," said Lola. "Not if you want to keep me here forever."

"I'm stuck here," she hissed, anger suddenly contorting her features. "And now you will be, too." The silence that followed the threat was deafening.

Fear sliced like a razorblade through Arlo's heart. "Look at her," he said, shocked by his own defiance. He was terrified, but every ounce of terror was now tinged with rage. He gripped Lola's hand and brought her closer to him, out of the shadow and into the moonlight.

"She's not one of you anymore. Can't you see we don't belong here? We're going now."

Hannah's crystalline eyes diffracted the moonlight, giving them an even more wicked appearance. They settled on Lola. She didn't move. None of them moved. And then bit by bit, in tiny increments, she seemed to come to the realization that Lola was not glowing—not a little—that her eyes and skin were opaque and dull.

And all at once she was filled with something Arlo couldn't quite decipher. Was it regret or recrimination? Desire or desperation? In any case, Hannah's whole body deflated.

"But . . . *how?*" she whispered, breaking the silence.

"Alice," said Arlo. "She helped us. She's gone now, too. We're leaving, Hannah. And you're not going to stop us."

Arlo straightened his spine. He took a few purposeful strides. He passed Hannah's small, defeated frame. She spared him a bitter, pitiless look and hung her head.

For a moment, it seemed as though she would let them go. She started to turn away, but then changed her mind. Her hand shot out like a whip. She grabbed Arlo's arm, clawing into it with white-hot needles, and like a volcano exploding venomous outrage, she screamed.

"They're here! They're here! Get them!"

The forest echoed with the hoarse cry of her resentment and fury. There was a rustle of shouting and movement far behind him.

Arlo wrenched his arm free. He squeezed Lola's hand and they began to flee toward the old sign and then onward along the road. He could see their car in the distance. It was covered in a thin layer of snow. He didn't look back.

Bodies appeared along the edge of the woods in his peripheral vision. They drew nearer, their twisted faces and glowing eyes filling the darkness.

His mother must have heard the commotion. She got out of the car, draped in various clothing, and began waving wildly.

"Arlo! Lola!" she cried.

The townspeople were behind him, beside him. There was no hope now. They would get to him and Lola and their mother. They'd drag them back to the town and then . . . And then what? Imprison them? Or worse?

Arlo's legs began to slow. There was a part of him that was too cold and too tired to fight. Too tired to take one more step. It was done. It was over. He could sense the glowing light around him. Enveloping him.

He was about to stop, to give up, when he took one

final glance over his shoulder. Lights were approaching. Two large circles of bright light. For a moment, he was perplexed, trying to make sense of what he was seeing. It wasn't glowing eyes. Or glowing bodies. And it wasn't the moon. It was nothing so wondrous, yet it was miraculous nonetheless.

25

As the headlights grew brighter and the SUV drew closer, the glistening bodies of the townsfolk retreated, melting back into the darkness of the forest wall. Arlo was elated, but still nervous, like he'd somehow won first prize in a contest by cheating.

The SUV slowed and then halted alongside him. Relief washed over Arlo as he recognized the contours of a familiar face. The window lowered, and his father's voice beat like a hollow drum in his ears.

"Arlo! Lola!"

"Dad!" he said breathlessly. "You came! You found us!"

"Dad!" echoed Lola. She hugged Arlo.

Arlo's father put the SUV into park and got out. He ran round the front just as Arlo's mother joined them.

She held Lola's face in her hands. "Are you okay? Is it done? Is it over?"

"Yes," said Lola. "Arlo did it! He saved me."

"Are you sure? Positive?" Tears glistened in their mother's eyes as the three fell together in a group embrace so hard, so close, Arlo was breathless with the force of it.

"How about you, Mom?" he asked, breaking free from the grasp.

"A bit cold," she chuckled. "But, hey—I eventually got a signal." She held up Arlo's phone. "And your father left right away."

"I came as fast as I could," he said, standing awkwardly outside the circle. "I'm sorry I didn't believe you, Arlo."

"It's okay," said Arlo, unable to keep the hint of resentment from his tone.

Before Arlo stepped away, his mother whispered, "How did you do it?"

He looked at Lola, then back at his mother. "I'll explain later."

"Let's get you to a hospital, Heather," said Arlo's dad.

"What about our suitcases?" she said. "Our clothes?"

Arlo glanced over his shoulder. There was a faint silverfish glow in the forest just beyond the line of trees.

He gulped. Words leaped from his mouth. "Forget it. It's just stuff."

"You're frozen," said Arlo's father, touching his mother's hand. He looked down at her cracked cast. "That looks horrible. Arlo was right. You need proper care. Let's find your purse. You can get the rest once a truck tows that wreck to a station."

He held open the front passenger door. She nodded and got inside. Arlo got into the back seat, followed by Lola. They stopped briefly at the wreckage.

"Wow," said Arlo's father, surveying the car up close. "You all were lucky you made it out of this alive." He choked on the last word, and then added quickly. "I'm really sorry. I should have come right away."

Arlo held his father's gaze and then nodded once. He wouldn't forgive him just yet, but it was a start.

Arlo's father found his mother's purse, then he jumped back into the SUV, and without further discussion, they sped off. His father was usually a man of few words, but he seemed to babble on endlessly, asking myriad questions, eliciting only vague responses as the landscape slid past. Arlo watched as the monstrous trees lining the road grew smaller and thinner.

The tide of emotions that had swelled inside him began to recede and at last left him feeling beached and dry. They had escaped Livermore, it was true, but glancing at his mother, her wounded ankle, her eyes exhausted and sunken, his heart stuttered in his chest, and he wondered if they'd made the right decision.

He was certain his mother's ankle would mend with proper attention, but then he thought of the scans and possible hard times ahead. What did the future hold? Uncertainty was the cruelest of all possibilities.

The car rolled along the narrow road and then turned onto a wider one. No one spoke for a very long while. Arlo remained awake, but Lola and his mother dozed.

Night began to blend with day as the first rays of sunshine reached up from below the horizon, chasing the darkness and making the gray clouds blush. Then at last, the sun appeared, and the whole landscape transformed.

They left New Hampshire and entered the state of Vermont. Arlo remembered the slogan he'd read on the New Hampshire welcome sign what felt like eons ago: Live Free or Die.

He hadn't understood its significance before. Yet, now its meaning was suddenly clear. The people of Livermore were not free. They were stuck, frozen in time forever. And that was not living. Not really.

His mother and Lola were awake again, though groggy. Reading his thoughts, his mother looked over her shoulder and reached a hand out to touch his knee. "Don't look back."

A lump rose in his throat as he gazed at her questioningly.

"Don't look back. Look forward, Arlo. Positive thoughts."

"Yeah, Arlo," echoed Lola between deep yawns. "Positive thoughts." She punched his upper arm and grinned.

As they headed back toward civilization, the town and his experiences there were already fading. Had it all truly happened? Or had they somehow imagined it? Now, in the clear light of day, so many miles away, it seemed too incredible a story to ever retell. Perhaps soon the town's inhabitants and the strange creature would become something confined to half memory, half legend in Arlo's mind.

Then, he suddenly remembered something. He reached into his pocket and withdrew the twig doll. He stared into the absence of its face. It was physically disgusting. He couldn't imagine what Lola had ever liked about it.

The spindly limbs and tangle of roots on the head reminded him of the hideous creature. What was it? Some ancient entity from another age? An alien? Would he ever know? Would it even matter?

Whatever it was, he'd decided, he'd leave it in peace. Let it live hidden from science and people that would harm it in order to understand.

He nudged his sister. She had been staring blankly out the window, lost in her own thoughts. The circle of tiny puncture wounds on her neck had already begun to scab over. She looked at him, then down at the doll. He placed it in her hands. She examined it momentarily, as though a trace of something fond still lingered.

Then she lowered the window. With two hands, she snapped the twigs in half and pitched them as far onto the side of the road as she could. She leaned back, put her soccer cleats onto the headrest in front of her, and closed her eyes.

Arlo smiled.

It's going to be okay.

They never told anyone about the townspeople or about the Nameless. They spoke of them only together, in hushed whispers, and as the years turned to decades, a curtain of silence seemed to close between them, making it more and more difficult to say the words out loud. Lola's scar, like the memory, faded over time, but never disappeared completely.

And though his recollection of the people and the events dulled and diminished, something had snagged in

Arlo's mind. He'd reach out for it now and then, in quiet moments, but it would evaporate before he could grasp hold of it. It was something about the town. Something about its name.

Livermore.

Livermore.

Live for more . . .

AUTHOR'S NOTE

I began writing the first draft of this novel so long ago, its working title was *Frozen*. Well, we all know what happened to that title . . . I'd go through several more titles before settling on *Shadow Grave*. I don't often write author's notes, but I feel compelled to tell my readers a little more about this story.

I'm often asked where my ideas come from, and my response, quite similar to most authors', is simple: everywhere. The compost of our imagination is teeming with life. It's a rich and fertile soil in which a seed, once planted, may flourish and grow. This particular story had several seeds, whose roots intertwined and whose shoots twisted to become this plot.

Seed number one: *Tuck Everlasting*. This brilliant work by author Natalie Babbitt lives up to its title in so many ways. From the time I read it, decades ago, its story and characters have remained with me. The novel gave me not only great pleasure but left me with large questions I shall ponder forever. If you have not read it—race to your nearest library or bookstore.

Seed number two: "The Road Not Taken," by Robert Frost. I love poetry. It's a personal experience—one to which you bring your own feelings and interpretations. Did Frost intend there to be a right path, a better path? The way I see it, life is an infinite series of choices that ultimately bring us to the same place: onward. We cannot stand at the crossroads forever, and so we must choose and hope for the best.

Seed number three: H.P. Lovecraft's stories, in particular, "The Nameless City" and "The Call of Cthulhu"—truly, the whole Cthulhu mythos, and the idea that there are things which lie beyond our human perception of reality. What did Lovecraft mean when he wrote *That is not dead which can eternal lie . . .* ? ("The Call of Cthulhu," 1928)

Seed number four: the tardigrade—sometimes called a *water bear* or *moss piglet*. While writing a nonfiction book on deserts, I came across these fascinating, bizarrely cute, and almost miraculous creatures. They are practically indestructible and can survive for decades without water or food. They can survive extreme temperatures, radiation, pressure equal to that of the deepest part of the ocean, and even the vacuum of space. Tardigrades will survive cataclysmic events that could wipe out most other species on this planet.

The fifth and final seed: Livermore. While the other four seeds lay dormant in my imagination, I happened to be engaging in one of my favorite pastimes—researching real-life ghost towns—when I came across this gem of a place—its remnants still hidden in the White Mountains of New Hampshire. I'd driven through New Hampshire many years ago and was struck by its solitude and beauty. I'd hoped to take the drive again in the summer of 2020, but, alas, the world had other plans . . .

Though little is left of the structures that were once this vibrant little logging town, it had a rich history. One timeline on the website bartletthistory.org suggested there may or may not have been forty people infected with smallpox and there may or may not have been a mass grave.

Though I have borrowed bits and pieces of the real town—its history, geography, a slightly altered name or two—*Shadow Grave* is wholly a work of fiction. Its inhabitants and the town are how I imagine them to have been—almost mythical.

In case you'd like to do a little ghost town research of your own, feel free to delve into Livermore. To get you started, enjoy the photograph below, courtesy of the Mountain Ear.

ACKNOWLEDGMENTS

A heartfelt thank-you goes out to the many people who helped make this story the very best it could be.

To my first-round readers—so generous with their time—Jaime Cohen, Michael Cohen, Cole Comia, Shalimar Santos-Comia and Debra Getts—your comments, questions, and encouragement propelled me onward.

To amazing author, Rebecca Upjohn, for lending her New Hampshire eyes to the manuscript and helping me with low walls, lichen, and all the beauty of the North Country.

To my wonderful family for their love and support while hours dwindled and dinners grew cold.

To the talented illustrator Hannah Peck for her exquisitely creepy cover—those colors!

To my agent extraordinaire, John M. Cusick, who, for more than ten years now, has been the wind in my sails.

To all the Roaring Brook staff, who work tirelessly to support my books: Connie Hsu, Kathy Wielgosz, Jennifer Healey, Trisha Previte, Morgan Rath, Emilia Sowersby, and Nicolás Ore-Giron.

And last, but most importantly, the biggest thank-you goes to my brilliant and kind editor, Emily Feinberg, for her wisdom and sensibility, for always nudging me gently in the right direction, and for loving creepy stories as much as I do.